FREEDOM SONGS

FREEDOM SONGS

Yvette Moore

ORCHARD BOOKS   NEW YORK

Orchard Books
A division of Franklin Watts, Inc.
387 Park Avenue South
New York, NY 10016

Manufactured in the United States of America
Book design by Mina Greenstein
The text of this book is set in 11 pt. Times Roman.
10   9   8   7   6   5   4   3   2   1

Library of Congress Cataloging-in-Publication Data
Moore, Yvette.
Freedom songs / Yvette Moore.   p.   cm.
Summary: In the sixties, when Sheryl's Uncle Pete joins
the Freedom Riders down South, she organizes
a gospel concert in Brooklyn to help him.
ISBN 0-531-05812-3.   ISBN 0-531-08412-4 (lib.)
[1. Civil rights—Southern States.   2. Uncles—Fiction.
3. Concerts—Fiction.]   I. Title.
PZ7.M788155Fr   1991   [Fic]—dc20   88-43073

□□□□□□□□□□□□□□□□□

For Rashad and Rashida; Rashon,
Rayona, and Kadeem; Teshonne,
Donnell, Dana, and Erica; for Shayla,
and Shani, and the children of
Lincoln Place. I love you.

With eternal love and gratitude for the
African-American Church. Special
thanks to the John Oliver Killens
Writers Workshop in Brooklyn.

NOTE ▣▣▣▣▣▣▣▣▣▣▣▣▣▣▣▣▣▣

In this book the term *Negro* is used instead of *black*.
In the 1960s, the time in which the story takes
place, *Negro* was the accepted term, used by
blacks themselves, and it has been used here for
historical accuracy.

1 ◻◻◻◻◻◻◻◻◻◻◻◻◻◻◻◻◻

Southern folk are mystical. Sirens and sounds from muf-flerless cars light up warm nights in Brooklyn where I live. But in my mother's North Carolina, prophesies drift on soft spring breezes alongside the scent of pine and honeysuckle, leaving little room for coincidence. Omen-filled dreams chart people's lives. They touch the intangible. Even when they leave the land, signs still follow.

For weeks in Mommy's dreams was her mother, smiling, walking, and surveying new surroundings. A brilliant sun beamed, but Ma Pudnum's face outshone it. For weeks Mommy told Daddy she had to go home to see her mother.

"It's just a dream, Ruby—don't worry," Daddy kept saying.

"I'm not worried—just want to see her," Mommy kept answering.

And so, in the wee hours of Good Friday morning 1963, we packed sandwiches and suitcases into our brown Bonneville and headed south, leaving in the middle of the night like fugitives making a clandestine return, to avoid traffic.

My baby brother, Ronnie, was most excited about the trip, it being his first time down and all. My older brother, Craig, said next time we should try to get Mommy to dream about Hawaii. Daddy swallowed the trip like a measure of castor oil—an occasional nasty necessity. For him southern air was saturated with bad memories of a sharecropper's son. Both his parents were dead when he left Alabama for the army, and he never looked back. Missed school days, and getting left back because he had to work some white man's farm, colored his South ugly.

For me North Carolina was cousins and fun, rainbow skies to sketch after sudden spring showers, and thick woods to explore on endless summer days. I loved being down there.

Daddy always looked at me and shook his head when I said I loved it down South. He'd "had enough of crackers to last a lifetime." "Crackers" is what he calls white folk down South. "Them" is what he calls white folk in New York. But that was Daddy's thing, and I didn't have time for it. And even if I did, I didn't know enough white people well enough to be calling them anything, really. The teachers at school were white, but they were teachers. And some of the shopkeepers around were white, but they were shopkeepers. There used to be some white kids on our block, but they moved away before I could even cross the street by myself.

Whatever Daddy said, *I* loved down South.

For one thing, people said my name right: Sheryl Williams. That's *Sheryl*, one syllable, like *Shirley* minus the *ey* part. Ever since kindergarten, teachers have been messing up my name. *She-ryl*, they'd always say. At first I corrected them, but they'd just look at me, smile crazylike, then say it wrong again. *She-ryl*'s not a bad name. It's just not my name. My name is *Sheryl*.

For another thing, down South could help me do the one thing I wanted to do by September, when I started high school—be a fly girl, a fly girl with lots of clothes and even more boyfriends. In every spare moment, and some not so spare ones, I image me in Wingate High School colors, red and white, pom-poms flying, cheering on the basketball team in the play-offs. Three minutes on the clock, they don't think they can pull it off. Then I start a cheer. The ball goes in, buzzer goes off, and they win by a point. Team lifts captain on their shoulders, but he's looking, looking, searching the crowd for something . . . somebody. . . . Me, because I'd be a fly girl by then.

Becoming one was going to be a full-time job in the four months I had left, as paltry as my wardrobe was and as strict as Mommy can be. But down South, I could at least practice. Who down there would know I wasn't a fly girl already? I had clothes enough to be fly for four days anyway. If I said something smart to a boy down there, who of my friends would be standing there to look at me like I'd sprung a leak through the top of my head? My cousins didn't know that in school I only daydreamed and went to art club. Even if they did, they wouldn't hold me to it. They'd let me try stuff, and on this trip, I would.

Craig, Ronnie, and I sat in the back of the car—Ronnie on my lap, looking out the window and asking if we were "down South yet" every five minutes; Craig stretching his long legs across the width of the car and over my ankles; I pressing my face against a backseat window, my drawing pad and pencil bag between my ankles. We sang with the radio, ate fried chicken, and played "my car" until we woke to the warmth of a rising cherry orange sun that I vowed to paint. Ronnie, after slobbering on my arm all night, was amazed to see grazing cows.

Yes, we were "down South yet," Mommy, now in the driver's seat, told Ronnie in baby talk.

"The mommy and daddy cows have to eat a go-od breakfast before they go to work, right?" said Ronnie, as serious as cancer. I tickled his ear with my nose.

"That *is* their job," Mommy said, "eating and being healthy enough to make good milk and more cows!" Daddy, still trying to sleep, put his hand over Mommy's mouth. She laughed and bit him. Mommy had shunned sleep all night, and now a numinous southern morning energized her.

Twenty minutes from Ma Pudnum's, Craig finally woke up and yawned.

"Ugh, boy, cover your mouth! Your breath smell like something dead's caught up in you!"

I pulled my sweater over my nose and quickly rolled down the window on my side. Craig laughed and stretched, then leaned over and blew his awful morning breath right into my face. I tried to push him back on his side. He tried to pull my sweater away from my face with one hand and roll the window back up with the other, all the time laughing and letting out more of that rot breath while Ronnie yelled about "horsies."

"Eh, knock it off back there—this ain't no playground." Daddy, abandoning the idea of sleep, sat up. He turned the radio back on, but only sad nasal voices backed by country

4

steel guitars filled the airwaves. We tried to make up sadder songs, but that was impossible.

And when the smell of burning wood filled the car, we knew the creek was near. Mommy screamed and opened the window to greet her mangy old friend. Local garbage was burned there, but for some reason the creek never smelled of burned rubble, just smoldering wood. Leaves had long since been seared off the dead and dying pines that stood scattered in bark-high creek water. We crossed the small bridge that overlooked the dank swamp, and its wobbly, weatherworn planks trembled under the weight of our car. I prayed it would stand, but Mommy didn't even slow down. When we screamed, she said, "Oh, hush, this bridge has been shaking ever since I can remember."

Well, that calmed our fears, Mommy.

Once over, we turned up the first dirt road, leaving a trail of dust behind us. Daybreak, and folk were already in their gardens, plowing their fields, or hanging out wet clothes. One by one, like molasses-covered dominoes, they'd stop to wave and try to figure who-all was in that honking car. Speeding, Mommy oohed and aahed, then named them with each honk: Miss Luella, Uncle Willie, Uncle Enoch, Cousin This, Deacon That. She went even faster after we crossed the railroad tracks.

Buds weren't even on Brooklyn trees yet, but spring flowers bloomed in Ma Pudnum's yard. Mommy tooted the horn and jumped out of the car into the arms of the smiling Dream Lady.

Ma Pudnum's nose had been itching—all week. Down South, everything meant something, and an itchy nose meant some unexpected body was on the way, but Ma Pudnum never figured it'd be her Ruby and us-all.

"Well, look-a-here," Ma Pudnum said, taking off her garden gloves. She pulled Daddy and Craig into her soft cheeks by the back of their necks.

"We down South!"

"Y'all sure are!" She picked Ronnie up and kissed him. "Do you know who I am, precious?"

"You my Puddin' Grandma!" Everybody cracked up at that.

Right about then, Ma Pudnum peered down into the car. "Where's Sheryl?"

I was in the rearview mirror, retwisting my ponytail as fast as I could.

"Good gracious," Mommy said, "is that girl still primping?"

Oh, Lord.

"Child, ain't nobody out here but us and the trees!" Ma Pudnum called. I took the curler out of my bang and got out of the car, smiling stupid and patting down my bang.

"Hi, Ma Pudnum!"

Ma Pudnum's eyes sparkled when she folded me into arms warm and smelling of sweet bread. The last time I hugged her, my head had rested right in the hollow between her round stomach and breasts. Now, my eyelashes brushed her cheeks. "Look at you!" Ma Pudnum said, stepping back to get a full look and to shine. "You done got all grown on me! How old are you now? Fifteen, sixteen?"

Fifteen, sixteen, ooh!

"Fifteen, sixteen? Lord, give me strength," Mommy said. "No, I'm fourteen."

"And looking just like Ruby when she was your age."

* * *

6

Being down South was nice, not only because folk say your name right, but because you see yourself at every turn. In New York, people say, although I don't see it, that Mommy, Daddy, and Craig, Ronnie, and I look alike. But to my eyes—and to Craig's too—there were missing links. Craig has the same eyes as Mommy, but where'd those big lips come from? Ronnie is the same Brazil-nut color as Daddy, but where'd he find those cheeks? Down South answered some of those mysteries. Take Craig's lips. We found them right in Ma Pudnum's room, hanging over her bed in an oil painting of Granddaddy tinted in subdued browns. Aside from the half-finished cigar gripped in the left corner of Granddaddy's mouth, those lips were Craig's.

(We also found the small, black potbellied stove, sitting on four legs next to Ma Pudnum's bed, that was responsible for the burn scar on Mommy's right cheek. Somehow when Mommy was about Ronnie's age, she fell onto one of the two small saucer-size circles directly on top of the stove, knocking into its long, large, ribbed, S-shaped pipe that ushered smoke up the chimney.)

Ronnie's cheeks and my nose we found in the middle of Ma Pudnum's face.

Ma Pudnum looks like an African-Indian. Surrounding her dark, supple, leather-baked face are two coarse gray braids pulled over the top of her head in opposite directions, pinned at the nape of her neck. Narrow Asianlike eyelids shelter dark round pupils that peer out over high cheekbones. Her large forehead, slanted like the side of a hill, was the same as Ronnie's. Small lips covered large china white teeth and firm jaws. In the middle of all that was my nose—and that made me happy as getting a gift when it wasn't even

Christmas. It made me think about all the other noses and lips and foreheads and cheeks and eyes and ears—especially the ones that couldn't be ignored—that I'd seen, in school, on the train. And I wondered who'd given those folks those features. And I wondered if they knew the family treasure laid open in the middle of their faces.

Sometime during all the hugging and inspecting, a tall, thin, young man in too-small overalls came out of the work shed. Mommy yelled, something about a college man in high waters, and ran for her baby, and only, brother, Peter. "Lord, have mercy," Mommy said. He was getting more handsome by the minute. They hugged and swayed. When they stopped, she looked up at him. "Do the girls ever let you study?"

"They let me get straight As." He smiled. But there was something in his eyes. . . .

Mommy's brother was nineteen and tall as Daddy, about six feet even, though much thinner, with skin smooth and dark as bittersweet chocolate. As for his face, I could see Mommy all in it—he was handsome. But his eyes were different. They were brown and almond shaped and covered with a thick canopy of black brows swerving this way, then that, like Mommy's—but something else was there. Mommy's eyes always danced on the edge of a smile, but his eyes were on the edge of . . . I don't know, something. Once when I was little and we came down here, I thought it was meanness and I decided to stay out of his way. But later that same stay, he came looking for me, offering a ride on the mule. I didn't even ask him, or Mommy, or Ma Pudnum, or anybody—I guess I must have looked like I wanted a mule ride. Anyway, his eyes weren't at meanness. They were . . . somewhere else. Even in laughter, they seemed focused light-years away. I wish I knew where.

Mommy's brother was a mystery to me. Not an evil, scary kind, but a mystery just the same. I just couldn't figure him out.

I didn't even know what I was supposed to call him. Seemed like he was just too young to call uncle, even though he was. Craig called him Pete, but Craig's two years older than me and there's only three years' difference in their ages. Usually, I didn't call him anything—just kind of threw my voice in his direction when I was talking to him. We didn't talk much anyway, so this more than sufficed. All he did was read and work; at least that's all I'd ever seen him doing. While they talked, I stared at him, even though I was trying not to, and wondered about his eyes.

"You still play football?" Craig asked.

"Yeah. We're training right now for next season."

School was out for Easter break, and Pete planned on setting out tobacco plants before the Good Friday sun rose high.

"I could help you with planting today."

"Sure—thanks."

Craig had volunteered for work—Lord, have mercy. We went inside to the other good thing about down South— Ma Pudnum's house.

From the outside it seemed small and simple, but inside a labyrinth of doors and rooms and closets where Craig and I used to play hide-and-seek told a story: This room was added when Mommy was born; that one when the baby got smallpox—it was turned into a sun porch when she died.

The large kitchen was one of the original rooms in the maze of seven in a house that had grown along with Ma Pudnum's family.

By the time we'd brought the luggage into the house and washed, breakfast was steaming on the table in the roomy kitchen—hominy grits and fried herring, buttermilk biscuits and homemade fig preserves, smoked ham and eggs to order. I had mine scrambled—hard. Daddy had his sunny-side up and oozing warm orange yoke all over the place. I put the milk jug between our plates.

Ma Pudnum always cooked for a legion, and that was a good thing too, because after she said grace and thanked God for the wonderful Easter surprise (that was us), neighbors and family began stopping by. They'd knock loudly on the front doorpost one or two times, then before Ma Pudnum could ever answer, the metal screen door would slowly screech open, then bam-slam shut just before the mosquitoes got in. The room broke into a million conversations, and the door kept screeching. Every time it did, I'd look up expecting to see Mommy's sister, Minnie Ruth, and her four daughters, but it never was.

After a while, Ma Pudnum's friend Miss Luella rose to take care of the million and two dishes piling in the sink. I offered to help, but she shooed me away like a fly. I didn't argue.

With all the clamoring in that kitchen, you could hardly hear Miss Luella clanking away with the dishes, let alone the person next to you. So how did everyone know to get quiet when Daddy, Craig, and Mommy's brother started talking about his school?

"Freedom riders? All that studying done made y'all crazy!" Ma Pudnum's brother, Uncle Willie, interrupted,

waving his hand at his nephew. "Besides, y'all want change right now. First off, white folk are never going to stand for it. And if they did oblige—and they won't—things take time."

"It's not *just going* to happen. We will make it happen," Mommy's brother said slowly. He controlled every syllable, but was angrier than I'd ever seen him; that much anger could not have been kindled just during the short time we had sat at breakfast. Was *that* behind those eyes—anger? Was it for white folk or Uncle Willie? The muscles around his jawbones tensed and relaxed, then tensed again. Uncle Willie ignored the comment altogether.

"Look, it could be worse. I've seen worse," he continued. "And if y'all keep messing with things, they're going to be worse. Messing with your *freedom riders* and their voting *rights* is what got that colored preacher's house bombed up by Goldsboro. What y'all young folks don't understand is that everybody has a *place* in life—"

My uncle jumped up from the table so fast his chair fell over backward. He stomped to the back door. The dishes in the breakfront trembled. He opened the screen door, but before he walked out, he turned back and glared at Uncle Willie.

"*I* say where my place is. *I* say where my place is." The screen door bam-slammed shut. Nobody knew what to say, so they all just kind of left, excusing themselves to go back to their work.

Whatever Mommy's dream had meant, it couldn't have involved her brother and his freedom riders, whoever they were, because rather than shining, Ma Pudnum's face had turned dull as used dishwater.

2 🔲🔲🔲🔲🔲🔲🔲🔲🔲🔲🔲🔲🔲🔲🔲🔲

There were no houses nearby. Oh, you could see a few at a distance, but nothing I'd call near. Still, walking was the only way I could go anywhere, since I didn't know how to drive. After breakfast Daddy went to sleep, Mommy and Ma Pudnum sat to talk, and Craig joined Uncle Pete in the field. I emptied the breakfast table scraps into the hogs' trough (what a mess!), then took Ronnie and set out for Aunt Minnie Ruth's.

Aunt Minnie Ruth lived three long blocks—well, something like blocks—away. Actually it was as long as three city blocks just to the end of Grandma's road, red as clay flowerpots and lined with towering evergreens. Tall cattails and weeds filled the ditches that separated road from trees. On the right side were thick woods, but on the left, behind a few trees, was a field that this year held peanuts and pigeon peas instead of tobacco like the rest. At the end of the road a small house sat in a clearing off the path in front of more trees.

"Is that Aunt Minnie Ruff's?" Ronnie asked.

"No, and I hope you're not tired, because I'm not carrying you."

"I'm not tired!" Ronnie smiled at me and tried to take bigger steps. I'd have slowed down, but not here. This was Clyde Dean's house, the only white man in this part of the village. They say he used to have a wife and lots of children. But now that his wife was dead and children gone, he had dogs. Lots of dogs that didn't like children. I picked up Ronnie just in case dogs really could smell fear. A big red one with its mouth wide open came from around the side of the house, as if I'd called it by name, and stared at us.

"Oh, oh, Sheryl, he thinks I'm breakfast and you're lunch," Ronnie whispered. The dog barked. From around the side of the house came a bigger black-and-white spotted dog. A black one crawled out from under the house. Ronnie wrapped his arms around my neck and his legs around my waist.

The dog growled. I jumped, almost dropped Ronnie. I picked up a piece of branch, but it was dry-rotted. "Tch, sugar!" The spotted dog was entering the ditch when an old brown pickup truck pulled up. I jumped on the side and pulled Ronnie into its empty back. It didn't matter who was driving. Around these parts it had to be some kin. And any direction away from those dogs was all right by me. We *almost* stopped at the stop sign by the fork in the road, then lurched to the right, zooming up Highway 64.

In less than five minutes, the truck slowed down, though not nearly enough, and jerked into Aunt Minnie Ruth's yard, shaking Ronnie and me up like dice. It barely missed hitting one of two white wagon wheels on both sides of the wood plank driveway spanning the ditch. We stopped with a sudden jolt that left no time for bracing. Still spinning, I climbed over the side of the truck in time to see long dungareed legs popping out the open driver door followed by a familiar face and a stranger's body.

Debra Jean? When had she outgrown me and become a bone? Her shoulders tried their best to cut right on through the Carter G. Woodson High School T-shirt she wore. Thank God, she had gotten rid of those funny-looking Pippi Long-stocking plaits that she loved so good and thought were so cute, that curled up like a flip at attention, that she put big old red ribbons on the end of, no matter what other colors she wore. Now, her sandy brown hair was pulled back into a single curled ponytail, displaying a round brown face, smooth and shiny as store-bought pecans.

"Ooh, Debra Jean, you look so different!"

Debra Jean sucked her teeth. "Save a person's life you haven't seen in four years, and she doesn't say, 'Thank you, How've you been?' Not even say, 'Hey, Dog.' Get back into the truck."

I went to hug my cousin, but she fanned me away. "Get away from me, you ungrateful hussy!"

Ronnie peered over the side of the truck. "Thank you!"

"Ah, this is little Ronnie!" She lifted him over the side of the truck and rocked him like a newborn.

Debra Jean's youngest sister, Terry Ann, came to the screen door hollering like the house was on fire. "Mama, come see what the wind blew in!"

"Girl, hush all that fuss 'fore they come cart you off to the state hospital!" Aunt Minnie Ruth was still talking when

14

she got to the door and saw us. "Lawd!" She let out a big yelping laugh, squeezed us tight, and landed loud kisses on both our faces. Her other daughters, Iris and Brenda, were with her.

"Mama, Clyde Dean's dogs were about to get them when I drove by just in time! I should have run one over."

"Next time," Brenda said, "you should try *not* to hit him. Then you can roll over him like you did Mama's rosebush."

"Oh, shut up."

"Debra Jean, when'd you learn to drive?"

"She didn't. Couldn't you tell?" Brenda said.

"You're only fourteen like me," I continued.

"Down here you can get a junior license at fourteen," Debra Jean said smiling.

"I see I'm going to have to have a word with that Clyde Dean about his devilish dogs," Aunt Minnie Ruth said.

When Aunt Minnie Ruth's husband died and she leased their land and enrolled in carpentry school, it was a Salisboro scandal. Folk said she'd ruin those girls of hers, acting like a man. She was pretty—surely some man would marry her if she'd act right, they said. The girls needed an example of how a woman should conduct herself, they said.

What they needed, Aunt Minnie Ruth answered, was dinner every night, clothes on their backs, and a roof overhead that didn't leak. Aunt Minnie Ruth threw her head back and started building cabinets. Now, three years later, a fragrant cross between pine and fresh-baked cinnamon rolls brushed my face as I entered the house readied for holidays. Crisp white ruffled curtains tied to opposite sides undulated softly with a breeze passing through the large picture window. Neatly tucked floral throw covers lay over the couch and adjacent love seat. An arrangement of Easter lilies sat on a lace doily on the handmade oak dining room table.

Aunt Minnie Ruth took Ronnie from Debra Jean and kissed him. When she knelt to put him back on the floor, her hand touched his behind. Ronnie's face dropped. Aunt Minnie picked him back up and left the room without a word.

"Let's get you a clean shirt," Debra Jean said. We passed a door ajar, and I glanced in.

"Oh, wow! A bathroom!" I yelled. No one had an indoor bathroom down here. Debra smiled but hesitated in answering.

"Yes and no. We can't afford the outside plumbing yet, but Mama has the indoor pipes in place." Well, no one could ever say they didn't have a pot to piss in. Covered in the corner of the new room was a big white pot with a red rim. A matching washbasin sat on a small white table pushed against the side wall. Four towels and facecloths hung side by side on two towel racks. Aunt Minnie Ruth had done it again.

Debra Jean searched neat dresser drawers for a shirt that would fit me. We had grown in opposite directions. Her baby fat had stretched to a thin strand with heaven on its mind. Mine, on the other hand, had just shifted.

"Try this one." She threw a short-sleeve white cotton shirt in my direction. The first three buttons closed fine, but my breasts wouldn't hear of that fourth one. I held my breath, rounded my shoulders, then gave up.

"How about a T-shirt?" Debra Jean was going through clothes in a second drawer as though they were top-secret files when Brenda walked in and said,

"I know you're not looking in your drawers for a shirt to fit Sheryl." She opened one of her drawers in a dresser on the other side of the room and took out a light blue shirt. "Face it, cousin, you've got the James tits. Only Debra Jean got off with those Taylor bumps!"

"I like it," Debra Jean retorted.

"Might as well," Brenda answered.

I stood, tucking the shirt into the top of my dungarees. Debra Jean was fussing with something on her dresser, looking in the mirror and doing something to her face. She turned around and smiled: mascara, cake powder, and pink lipstick. She turned back to the mirror. Brenda and I rushed to her sides and stared at her mirrored image even though we were standing next to the real thing.

"I just bought this stuff uptown," Debra Jean said proudly. "What do y'all think?"

Brenda moved closer to the mirror. "You look dead!" Debra Jean turned to strike, but Brenda cut her off. "No, really, Debra Jean, I'm not trying to be funny! Close your eyes." She closed her eyes, and Brenda crossed Debra Jean's arms over her chest. "Sheryl, can't you see that in a casket?"

A chill went through me—she was right. "Try it without the powder," I said. There used to be a lady in our church in Brooklyn who looked the same way. I think she really is dead now, though. Boy, that's rough, to be walking around half your life looking dead, then have to turn around and die.

Debra Jean left to get water and came back scrubbing her face with what had been a white facecloth. Now it was covered with fox red powder. That stuff may have looked like chalk, but it didn't come off that way. Gook was still on her face, and no more clean spots on the rag, when Debra Jean said, "Whew, I'm tired."

I got some soapy water and tried to scrub Debra Jean's face hard, but her head kept moving, so Brenda held it still.

"Ouch! That hurts!" Debra screamed, trying to wring free.

Brenda held tight. "This stuff's got to get off your face before it sinks in and dries!"

"Okay, but watch out for my eyes! Don't let soap get in my eyes!" And so, of course, soap promptly got into her eyes.

"Aaaaa!" Debra Jean jumped up and down, shaking her hands, screaming. We rushed her to the kitchen, where Iris was fixing to clean vegetables.

"Move, Iris! This is an emergency!" Brenda shouted, and Iris swung out of the way. We splashed away until Debra Jean's screams in pain turned to pleas for us not to drown her. And after all of that, her face was still red. Or was her skin raw now?

"What in the world are y'all doing?" Iris said, peeking over at Debra Jean. There was still mascara around her eyes. "Trying to take makeup off or skin?" She shook her head and went to her room, coming back with a large jar of cold cream that she massaged into Debra Jean's face. Now, with soft tissues, red gook and black mascara slid right off. "All you had to do was ask, Debra Jean, and I would have fixed up your face."

Iris muttered something about the blind leading the blind and invited us into her room. Everything was either pink or white—the walls, the bedspread, the curtains. That was too much for me. Over her bed hung a lightly painted photograph of a soldier in army fatigues and a helmet marked

AIRBORNE. He was overseas in a place called Vietnam that was something like China, she said.

Iris wanted to do my face first, since I was something like company and Debra Jean's face was sore. She sat on the bed, I on a chair in front of her, and Debra Jean and Brenda at my sides. I closed my eyes and felt her run a pencil along the lids. I felt like a piece of sketching paper.

"Open your eyes." She tilted her head and stared, her thumb and forefinger holding the pencil and her chin. "Okay, close them again." I could feel the line being extended and turned up at the corners like pictures of Cleopatra. She put color on my bottom lip, then said, "Do like this," folding her lips together. She dabbed my nose with a dry rubbery sponge. "Finis!"

"No powder?"

"No, the powders are either too light or too red for our color skin. We look better like this," she said, and snapped her lipstick back in its holder. "Now Debra Jean might be able to use some powder, but not that red she has."

Debra Jean, Brenda, and I gaped at the stranger in the mirror that was me. That girl did not play double dutch or draw willows. She was . . . a fly girl. I patted my bangs down. She wore stockings every day and didn't cross the street to avoid passing a group of strange boys. And, oh, God, she liked to dance the "grind"—I could feel it. Debra Jean and Brenda felt it too—I could see it in their eyes.

Sun-baked clay roads, dry and hard like pots in a kiln. But the ground was damp and air cool underneath the covering of the piney woods' dense branches. Aunt Minnie Ruth had taken the truck, leaving us to walk back, but this time our cousins guided us along a wooded route that bypassed those dreadful Dean dogs. After about ten minutes of walking, we could see the back of Clyde Dean's house a short distance away through the trees. Spot was terrorizing the other pups.

"Be real quiet," Iris whispered. She lifted her skirt almost to her waist and carefully stepped over a barbed-wire fence. "Don't touch this fence—it's hot."

"It doesn't look hot," I said.

"If you touch it, a bolt of electricity will light you up like a bulb!" Iris warned me.

"Clyde Dean put it up to keep his cow from roaming off," Debra Jean explained. "Soon as it got warm this year, he ran this line all the way around what he thinks is his property. Only not all of what he wired off is his. Some of it is Ma Pudnum's."

"Hush, before those dogs see where we are," Iris said. Debra Jean lifted Ronnie over the fence, and Iris took his hand. We followed. The ground was no longer damp, but soggy. I was barefoot, and this was disgusting. Mud and moss oozed up between my toes, lapping over the big one like a ring. Clyde Dean's hot wire ran a jagged path. We crossed it so many times, I gave up trying to figure out whose side we were on.

"So what's this about the fence being on Ma Pudnum's land?" I asked.

"Last year when Ma Pudnum was having timber cut, Clyde Dean came out shooting at the work crew and telling them to get off his land," Brenda answered. "Ma Pudnum went out to him, talking nice and everything, trying to show him the deed. Well, he cursed out heaven and all its hosts and told Ma Pudnum he didn't need to read no deed—not that he could—to find out where his land was.

"Lucky for Ma Pudnum the men had already done what

20

they were going to do, because when the sheriff came, he told her she couldn't cut any more timber until Clyde Dean came around or the court settled it. Ma Pudnum was steady showing him the deed in her hand, but he acted like he couldn't read either.

"Petey tried to get Ma Pudnum to take him to court, but she wouldn't. She was scared because in court with deed in hand was where Arthur Brown lost about half his land to Clyde Dean, who had no deed at all. The judge said Mr. Arthur waited too long to say anything about it and gave the land to Clyde Dean."

"What?" I said.

"That's the law down here," Iris said. "If someone is openly using your land as their own and you know about it but don't contest it in court, after twenty years it legally becomes the other person's.

"But Clyde Dean himself may have saved Ma Pudnum's land by putting up these very wires. Ma Pudnum saw this wire line and had a righteous fit! When she finished, she told Pete to take care of it!"

"So why are the wires still up?"

"The judge said we had to get a surveyor to walk out the deed and mark the proper boundaries," Iris said.

An open field that led to Ma Pudnum's house was visible through the trees. Soggy soil was now covered with big puddles of water. Debra Jean put Ronnie on her back as Iris threw a thin fallen tree trunk across the biggest puddle. Debra Jean walked in the water, ignoring Iris's makeshift bridge.

"Iris."

"Yes?"

"Does Pete . . . Uncle Pete . . . like Uncle Willie?"

I spread my arms for balance and walked the trunk as

though it were a circus tightrope, even over slimy moss that covered half the bark near the center. I almost slipped on that mess, but I grabbed hold of something instead: the hot wire. A hum so deep it moved the earth shuddered through me.

Energy flowed into ankle-deep muddy water that rippled like a pebble-hit pond. I heard my mind scream *Move!* but my strength had drained into the water. *Move!* mind said again, but my leg refused. Cool hands cupped my face.

"Sheryl, Sheryl, are you all right? Sheryl!" Iris gently tapped my cheeks. I thought about answering yes, but my mouth was just too tired. *Well, then, at least nod. They're worried!* Sure enough, Iris's brown eyes were darting voraciously over my face, searching for signs of well-being. *Now, don't you feel silly? You're fine—tell her so!*

"Hum, hum" used all the strength my voice could muster. Iris took my hand. We walked through ankle-deep muddy water, then on across an open field sprouting bluets and dandelions turning into feathery wishes. We passed the wide weeping willow, its viny leaves blowing in the wind like white folks' hair. More and more, the steady gust and chirping birds made Iris's questions, which I was too tired to answer, seem ridiculous: "What's your name, Sheryl? Where do you live? What's your mother's name?" Inside I knew it was my own fault, since I hadn't answered her reasonable questions.

"I'm fine, Iris, really. Just sleepy. Very sleepy," I think I said. We climbed the three short steps up Ma Pudnum's front porch. I collapsed on Mommy's old bed amid voices concerned for me and angry about the hot wire. The voices became fainter and fainter until I was alone in a dark empty movie theater showing no film.

3 □□□□□□□□□□□□□□□□

Craig and Ronnie had tried, but I just knew they were part of a dream. Then Mommy pried my eye open with a light. That woke me.

"Mommy!"

"She's all right!" she shouted to the rest of the house, and snapped off the flashlight. "Get up, Sheryl. We're going to church."

"Ooh, God." I sank back into the pillow. Mommy went out and came back with soap, towels, and water in a small tin washtub. Clyde Dean's fence zapped me, but it didn't kill me. No way in the world Mommy was going to let me skip church on Good Friday night, tired or not. I got up.

"Mommy, about what time you think we'll get out?" The wall clock showed a little after six.

"We'll get out when the Spirit say we get out."

Oh, Lord.

At our church in Brooklyn the deacons prayed for the Spirit to come into the service, gave it about two hours to get there, and after that, come or no, we left. Down here, they waited, and waited, biding time with testimonies and singsongy prayers that weaved in and out of choruses. I don't mind going to church, but I mind staying all night, or all day, especially in the summer when the sun's shining, all bright, calling you to come be in it, and you're stuck in church waiting for a Spirit that anybody with eyes could see was outside enjoying the sun. *Lord, please come quick tonight.*

I washed fast, before the water could get cold, and put on a white dress for communion. I started to wear socks so I wouldn't have to fiddle with nylon seams, but I didn't.

"Sheryl, hurry up!"

The bad thing about people knowing how to say your name right is that they use it too much.

Debra Jean nudged me to tie the white kerchief she'd passed me on my head. I put it on like Debra Jean had done hers—so the bangs lay down right.

"Really, our hair's not supposed to be showing at all," she whispered, not missing a clap beat to the chorus.

"Look, we got them on our heads, right?"

"Yeah."

"All right, then."

Debra Jean laughed.

Night air was thick and still in the small wooden church building nearly a century old. I tried to stir it up some with the Jones Funeral Home hand fan from the hymnbook slot in front of me. But there was more to this air than a breath, and it would only move by will of spirit. I fanned in vain till a voice that rose from the sea of white dresses and scarfs to the right of the pulpit shifted the air. That's where the older women, the Mothers of the church, sat. A short, stout Mother, her feet barely touching the floor, tilted her head to one side as though listening, then issued a sound that flowed from her belly like endless waves of warm water. The current overpowered the church and swept us into its song.

> "Cal-va-ry-ee!
> Ca-al-va-a-ry-ee
> Surely He-e died on
> Cal-va-ry."

The stomp of heavy feet against wood floor planks marked the downbeat in the slow-moving dirge that made my heart pound. I helped keep the words and melody while a handful of folk wrapped flatted seventh moans and other harmonies around it so tight my eyes watered. Ma Pudnum was a flat wrapper. With her eyes closed, minor arpeggios leaped out of her mouth as a somber procession of deacons passed around a plate filled with flat homemade bread torn to pieces. A deacon, in a deep raspy voice, began the communion litany.

" 'The Lord Jesus, the same night in which he was betrayed, took bread . . .' "

Debra Jean and I were singing and swaying like old ladies till the communion plate stopped with us. Debra Jean liked communion bread; I didn't.

"I want a big piece," she whispered.

"They're all big. Let me break off some from yours."

"Uh-uh. Take some off that one."

25

The deacon whispered, "Move the plate on! What' the matter with y'all? 'And when he had given thanks, he brake it and said, "Take, eat: this is my body which is broken for you." ' "

I broke some off that other piece of bread. We sang until bread was in each palm, then ate the dry, tasteless bits together.

White hairs strained from under her scarf when the little Mother once again leaned her head to the right. I closed my eyes to see if the soft contours of her face would come out best in pencil or chalk. She listened and sang.

> "Can't you he-ar Him
> Cal-lin' Hi-is Fa-thah?
> Surely He-e died on
> Cal-va-ry."

Ma Pudnum resumed her rock and the deacons their march, this time with a large metal cup.

" 'Jesus, pouring the fruit of the vine, said, "This is the new testament in my blood. . . ." ' "

The little Mother continued the chorus, and they passed the cup around.

"We all gonna drink out the same cup?" I whispered.

"Yeah."

"With all of these no-toothed people?"

Debra Jean jabbed my leg, but it was true. The church was full of toothless wonders. And I bet most of them that had some teeth chewed tobacco, or worse, dipped snuff. Both kept a mouth full of juicy, stringy, brown spit. Almost every house you went to down here, you had to be careful not to knock over spittoons made from old Maxwell House coffee cans sitting near corner chairs. A snaggle-toothed flat wrapper stopped singing to sip. She passed the cup to Debra Jean, and Debra Jean to me. Small bubbles clung to the insides of the cup; two bigger ones overlapped each other.

The deacon looked at me like, "You gonna take communion tonight or tomorrow?"

I closed my eyes and sipped. "Oh, my Jesus."

The deacon said, "Praise Him, baby girl."

> "Can't you he-ar
> The ha-a-mer-ers ring-ing?
> Sure-ly He-e died on
> Cal-va-ry."

The deacon went on with the litany, but this part was more like a conversation between him, the Mothers, the flat wrappers—the whole church.

"Jesus knew that the time had come for him to leave this world and to go to the Father."

"My Lord!"

"He loved his own who were in the world. He decided to show them the full extent of his love."

"Uh-huh!"

"So he got up from the meal, took off his outer garment, and began to wash his disciples' feet."

"Yes, he did!"

"Now, when he got around to Peter, Peter said, 'Lord, are you going to wash my feet?' "

"Well!"

"Peter said, 'No, Lord. You'll never wash my feet like some old servant.' But Jesus had a surprise for him. He

27

said, 'If I wash thee not, Peter, you'll have no parts with me.' ''

"Mercy!"

"Well, Peter changed his mind quick, fast, and in a hurry! He said, 'Lord, not my feet only, but also my hands and head!' Let us do likewise."

> "I feel better,
> So much better,
> Since I laid my burdens down."

I always liked foot washing, though I don't really know why. Maybe because hardly any other church did it. Our church in New York did, but only because it was connected to this little church hidden in the woods down here. Friends laugh when I tell them about it. They ask if the people's feet are real dirty, if they smell, and, of course, why don't folk wash up at home. But I always liked foot washing. It was like initiation into a secret society or something.

The men and boys moved up to the choir loft while the women and girls paired off in the rear pews. Fat ladies went to the bathroom, because taking off stockings is a chore when you're wearing a girdle. Slumped down in my seat, I unfastened my garters and carefully rolled down my stockings. I walked barefoot to the front of the church, where the little Mother who led the singing poured water into basins. Her song went on even when she stopped pouring to smile and beckon me dip my feet into the basin before her. She knelt at my feet. Now, that didn't seem right. Usually I washed feet with somebody my own age like Debra Jean, or maybe even as old as Mommy. But this old woman kneeling at my feet . . . I just glazed the bottom of my feet in the water so they wouldn't get too wet and she could hurry up and get up. She didn't go for it. She pushed my feet down into the basin and washed them. *Oh, boy.* Well, I'd be sure to do her feet good too. After she dried my feet with the long towel wrapped around her waist, I helped her loosen the towel and tied it around my own waist. She sat on the front pew and placed her tiny feet in the basin. How soft the dark, wrinkled skin was! I poured handfuls of tepid well water over them and massaged them the best I knew how. She smiled. I toweled them dry. Between choruses she pointed to basins of water, motioning me to take them to the women in back who were now ready to wash feet. She followed me, carrying an armful of long towels.

And the women washed feet. Mommy rubbed her mother's right ankle where arthritis always tried to set in. On her knees, Aunt Minnie massaged the feet of a heavy, brown-skinned lady whose singing mouth revealed scattered tobacco-stained teeth. The woman was older than Ma Pudnum but had two long braids hanging over both her shoulders like a little Indian girl. A young white-looking woman—I knew she couldn't have been white because no white people came to this church—washed Debra Jean's feet. She kept pushing back long, loose, sandy hair that was determined to fall in the basin.

In the choir loft the men had taken off suit jackets and rolled up white dress-shirt sleeves. Uncle Willie popped his suspenders in time to the chorus and rested his head on the back wall as Mommy's brother dried his feet. Daddy washed Craig's feet, then Ronnie's. All the while, no one spoke, just sang.

As the women finished, Debra Jean helped me take the

basins back up front to empty into a large bucket. We slipped our stockings back on and took seats up front. The deacon gave the final word. "Now sometime during the meal, the disciples started arguing about which of them was the most important, and Jesus was just sitting there listening."

The church followed his lead with a familiar refrain of gasps, "Mercy, Lord" and "Uhn, uhn, uhn" uttered as though the story had never been heard before.

"And when he couldn't take anymore, he told his disciples, 'Kings rule over the people of the world, telling them to do this, telling them to not do that. But that's not how you're supposed to be.' "

A chorus of syncopated nos welled up and fell over.

"Instead," the deacon continued, "the greatest among you should be like the youngest!"

"Yes!"

"And the one who rules, like the one who serves!"

"Say so, Deacon!"

"Jesus told them, 'Tonight, I set an example for you.' "

"And a good one too!"

" 'You call me Teacher and Lord—and you're right because I am—but I live alongside you as a servant. If I have washed your feet, you should wash one another's feet.' "

The little Mother jumped up out of her seat shouting that on earth God had "no hands, but my hands; no feets, but my feets!" For the next five minutes, she walked swiftly up and down the middle aisle, shouting her refrain and showing God her hands and her feet.

When she finished, the church got quiet. We sang a hymn and left.

The silence broke again as greetings went out and the small crowd headed for the door. Outside, Mommy's brother and Craig started talking to a white-looking guy about their age. This was strange. Who was he? Debra interrupted my thoughts, appearing around the side of the church grinning and holding something wrapped in a napkin.

"Extra bread. Hmm!" she said.

"You like that stuff?" I asked.

"I love it!" She tore a piece, popped it into her mouth, then tried to hand me a piece. "Want some?"

"Ish!" I turned my head away. "Hey, who was that washing your feet tonight?"

"I don't know. Never saw her before." Debra took another bit of bread from the napkin. "When you went up front and washed Mama Hemby's feet, I turned around to find another partner, and she was standing there."

"She white?"

"You blind? Of course she is. Look at her."

"Isn't that strange?"

"Strange? Well, I don't know. It *is* Good Friday."

But it was strange. Anyone who just wanted to go to church on Good Friday would never find this place. Back Creek is not a country church that you pass off the side of the road on the way to anywhere. Only a use-made path leads to the meeting house adjacent to a yard filled with weatherworn headstones and planks marking graves that date back to antebellum times. It's way back in the woods, as though the builders were trying to hide it.

When Debra wandered off in search of extra grape juice, I started toward the small circle that had formed around Mommy's brother, a circle that included the girl who had washed Debra's feet. "Sheryl, Sheryl, come here!" Ma Pudnum grabbed my hand, pulled me under her arm, and turned to her friends. "This is my Ruby's girl." I smiled, but not much; if I looked too interested, I'd never get away from them.

"Is that right?" said one, smiling. "Well, I remember the night your mother was born." *Oh, Lord, here we go.* The circle around Mommy's brother had grown quite intense, with lots of hand gestures and slow nods. I had to get over there.

"Come over here, child," said another, this one squinting. "Let me see if you favor your pretty mama or that ugly daddy of yours." They laughed. Ma Pudnum playfully hit the woman but didn't let go of me.

"Don't you call my son-in-law ugly!"

The woman feigned shock. "Well, Pudnum, what do you want me to call him?"

"Robert," Ma Pudnum said. "Okay, Sheryl, you can go on now. You're wiggling so."

I dashed away. But before I could get to the circle, it began to rain. Everyone scattered. The two whites jumped into a light blue Bel-Air and headed down the road.

Hodges' five-and-ten-cent store bustled on the Saturday before Easter. Last-minute everythings were being purchased—a purse to match, a picture to hang, a tablecloth to spread. Miss Luella needed new white gloves to wear with her new rose-print dress and asked Mommy's brother to take her to town to shop. Craig, Ronnie, and I went along for the ride.

Hodges' was a funny old store. Who ever heard of being able to buy a quart of milk and a television set in the same place? But that's how it was at Hodges'. Some of it no one wanted—like the guitar wrapped in a yellowing plastic bag—but it was there. House shoes and hamburgers, dresses and duck-hunting whistles. Hodges' had everything.

Something for everyone, including Miss Luella. Mommy's brother and Craig followed Miss Luella's quick, deliberate steps toward an enclosed glass counter filled with gloves in the back. I checked out the watercolor paints in the stationery and art supplies section. Ronnie took off for a green and white water fountain too high for him to reach.

"Sheryl, I want some water," he called. I glanced up to see Ronnie on his tiptoes trying to climb the fountain. I put the paint set down and went to his aid, passing a woman who immediately stopped examining head scarfs to stare at me. I picked Ronnie up and stepped on the fountain's floor pedal. Ronnie drank some and stopped.

"This water tastes funny, Sheryl," he said, then drank some more.

"What are you doing?" the scarf woman finally said.

"He's too small to reach the fountain," I answered. What a stupid question. Had she been my age, I'd have answered, "Sleigh riding," but she was as old as Mommy, so I explained the obvious. She scurried up the aisle like a madwoman with all the scarfs in her hands.

I had put Ronnie down and was drinking myself when a heavy male voice boomed and made me jump. "Hey, what are you doing?"

He took long, heated strides in my direction. I looked around to see who he was talking to. I didn't see anybody else, and he was still coming in my direction, so I moved out of his way.

"What are you doing?" he said again, looking straight into my eyes.

"Drinking water." I wiped my mouth with the back of my hand and stepped back.

"Where're you from?"

"Brooklyn."

"Well, this is North Carolina, and that"—he pointed to the water fountain—"is for white people, not nigras."

"Excuse me? I am Negro." I felt my eyes start to blinking fast.

"I don't give a damn what you call yourself—just don't drink out of this fountain again." He wiped the fountain out with a white rag and ammonia and left.

My eyes blinked faster. Curses rushed my brain and jammed my throat, coming out only in sputters and grunts. A hum so deep it moved the earth shuddered through me.

"Come on, Sheryl."

Had Hodges' been this way all the time? How had I missed it all these years? I tried to think back. *Nigra! That man looked me in my eye and called me* nigra! *What kind of word was that? Is that the same as* nigger? *Of course it is, stupid. Maybe that's how he pronounces* Negro. *No, no—he meant* nigger. *And he meant* me. *He wiped out the fountain with ammonia, as if we had contaminated it!*

Ronnie took my hand. "Come on, Sheryl."

"Fat wombat."

The woman with the scarfs gasped.

In the back, Miss Luella, sucking her teeth and shifting her little bit of weight to her left leg, examined gloves. Craig leaned against a table of house shoes with his arms folded. I came up behind him and stood close.

"Craig."

"Huh? Where you been?"

"Boy, you better get me out of here."

"You want something?"

"I want to go home. All the way home."

Thick cotton gloves were too plain for a woman like her, Miss Luella said half to herself. Those new nylon stretchy ones were for a child, she complained. But, oh, those over there—she pointed to lace with beaded roses at the wrists—those were her.

Two women were ahead of Miss Luella in line for service. After trying on every glove in the case, the first woman bought the nylon stretch pair, vowing to bring them back if they cut off her circulation. The second woman knew what she wanted—the thick boring cottons.

"How do, Miss Hodges," Miss Luella said sweetly to the young woman tending the counter.

"Fine, thank you. And how are you, Luella?" the young woman said, using a mouthful of southern *R*s and flat vowels.

"I'm farin' right fine, thank the Lord. I'd like to see those beautiful lace gloves with the beaded roses."

As Miss Luella spoke, a woman came to the counter. "I'll be right with you, Luella," the shopkeeper said, and walked down the counter to the other woman.

Get out of here! I knew that lady wasn't going to leave Miss Luella and serve somebody else! I punched Craig in the back. "Did you see that?"

"I clocked it."

"Hey, lady!"

"Shush!" Craig said.

"Don't shush me! You saw what she did!"

"I want to see this."

"I've seen enough!"

I started to walk away, but I made a U-turn. I didn't want to see it, but I had to.

"I declare, Helen! I'll never know why I always wait to the last minute to do things!" the new customer said.

"Well, we're right here, ready when you are, Mary Beth!" They both laughed from the mouth.

"I'll tell you what—you can give me two pair of those flesh-tone stockings that I like so much—you know the ones I mean," said the customer.

"I sure do!" The shopkeeper searched her stock, then pulled down a box full of stockings from the second shelf. "Here we go," she half-whispered. Helen put the stockings into a white paper bag. "That'll be one dollar, Mary Beth."

The woman paid her. "Helen, you saved me again! Have a happy Easter!"

"Now, Luella, what did you say you wanted?" the shop-keeper said as two girls a little older than me approached the counter, giggling. She broke off. "Betty Sue and Caro-lyn, are you girls enjoying your day?" The shopkeeper left Miss Luella pointing at lace gloves in an enclosed glass case. The girls wanted garter belts. I wanted to scratch all of their eyes out.

"Miss Hodges, we'll take those gloves now and be going," Mommy's brother said evenly. The shopkeeper turned around.

"Why, Petey, you see I have my hands full with all of these customers today. I'm doing the best I can!"

"You're not *giving* Miss Luella gloves. She's buying them. So, we'll just take those gloves now and be going," he said. The girls stopped laughing and chewing.

"Why—" The glass doors behind the case nearly shattered as the shopkeeper angrily slid them back. She threw the lace gloves into a bag.

I punched Craig again.

"Check the size, please," Mommy's brother said in the same steady voice. The girls whispered, trying to figure out who Mommy's brother thought he was.

"What size do you take, Luella?" she said coldly.

Miss Luella glanced at her small hands, cinnamon brown and wrinkled by years of washing clothes.

"I'll give you a medium. You know you can't try them on." She threw a pair into the bag. "That'll be two sixty-five." Miss Luella gave her three dollars. She slammed change on the counter. Pete took Miss Luella's arm and led her out the store. We followed.

I stopped at the water fountain and spit in it.

Excluding noise from a loose muffler and Ronnie singing, the ride back was quiet.

4 ◻◻◻◻◻◻◻◻◻◻◻◻◻◻◻◻◻

Birds were still sleeping when I woke dark and early Easter morning. I gathered the covers around my neck, snuggling into the spot I had warmed during the night, and thought about going to the bathroom. *You're at Ma Pudnum's.* Just like that, it came to me. I smiled, till I remembered what that meant in bathroom terms: the outhouse.

My eyes stretched and blinked, straining to make out something, anything, in the pitch-black that silenced the room. I couldn't see my hands, let alone a small slop pot hiding in a shadow. I felt on the table next to the bed for the flashlight Mommy had used to wake me up for church the other night and found it. There's something to be said for not putting things away. I switched it on and panned its narrow beam across the room and over the side of the bed, head upside-down looking under the bed. But no slop pot.

Oh, brother.

Just make like you're camping in the woods. Make like?

The wood floor was cold against the tips of my toes. Quickly I pulled on socks and threw on pants and sweatshirt on top on my pajamas. All that moving made me want to go more, and bending over to tie my sneakers didn't help the matter. I dashed out the room, grabbing a handful of napkins off the kitchen table on the way out the back porch door, just in case.

Night covered like a lead blanket snuffing light, swallowing sound. Barely visible were the silhouettes of trees, chicken coop, shed. My light was so small against this darkness. *Hey, are you scared? No. But, God, does it really need to get this dark? What if somebody grabs you? The night would soak up your screams like a packed closet.* Then I'd go on him.

Dawn doesn't really break—it spreads . . . like ink in a glass of water. The sky was no longer black, but navy blue with crystal chips spewn across it. Ma Pudnum's back porch faced east, where light would soon wipe gentle hues over the stars. I got my pad and chalks and a quilt, then came back to the porch swing to watch and wait. Sitting sideways with my feet up in the swing, I gripped the flashlight between my knees and lightly sketched the subtle line of outhouse and trees against the sky. A hush that covered the dawn helped me hum the call to worship chant from Habakkuk that we used in youth fellowship.

> But the Lord is in His holy temple;
> Let all the earth keep silence before Him.

Truly, the morning was silent. Still, with no sound but the slight squeak of the swing and a crunch, crunch over by the shed. *Keep silence*. Crunch, crunch, thump! I stopped the swing with my foot and turned off the flashlight. Somebody was walking over by the shed! The door slowly whistled open, and the light inside went on. The crunching footsteps came out with a high-beam hand light.

It was Uncle Pete! What was he doing up this early on Easter?

He opened the hood of the truck, shining the light all around. He touched and yanked, then slammed the cover back down. He twisted himself under the truck on his back. Was he trying to repair it? But he had no tools, only that light.

After a while he squiggled back out. Now he was crawling on his hands and knees, searching all around the wheels. Where he couldn't see, he felt with his hands. For what? Finally, he got in the truck and started the ignition. But something told me he wasn't going anywhere. Sure enough, he turned off the ignition, hopped out, and went to the tractor just inside the shed. The view was not a straight one, but I could see him starting that same exam on the tractor. Soon the engine revved. Then it cut off, and he crunched back out. Dew-moistened grass hit against his heavy work boots as he headed for our car!

Something was wrong. The sky was royal blue now, and the birds had begun their morning song. I pulled the quilt over my head and settled back into the swing and watched him probing, poking, jabbing that light under the hood, around the wheels. He stood up and tried the doors. Locked. We always locked our doors—even down South. He studied our car, walked around it, rapped his fingers over the top. He opened the hood and looked again, then backed away into the shed. He came back with a wire. He opened the door to our car. Something was really wrong.

And just like that it came to me, Uncle Willie's voice at Friday morning breakfast.

"Messing with your freedom riders *and their voting* rights *is what got that colored preacher's house bombed up by Goldsboro."*

That was it! God, that was it!

Uncle Pete sat in our car longer than the others, but finally it started too! Mellow streaks of violet highlighted flat, peaceful baby blue clouds, while Uncle Pete checked for bombs. My heart banged. He crunched back to the shed.

You better get off this porch before he finds out you've been out here spying on him. I wasn't spying on him! Run in the house while he's still in the shed. The light went out in the shed. I heard him come out. *Sketch something real fast so he won't think you've been looking at him all this time.* But I'd have to turn the flashlight back on. *God, please let him use the front porch.* He moved toward the back porch. *Play possum. That's stupid. So? But why would I be sleeping outside on the swing?* Crunch, crunch. *Why would you be spying on somebody before the sun came up?* Crunch, crunch. *Oh, God, please don't let him be mad.* A bomb? How could I ever look him in the eyes again? I opened my eyes.

"Hi. It's me, Sheryl." I shined the flashlight in my face and smiled like an idiot. He stopped about ten feet from the porch. I should have played possum.

"Sheryl? What are you doing out here?"

"I went to the outhouse and stayed to watch the sun come up."

"Why didn't you use the slop pot in your room? You don't come out the house in the middle of the night to go to the bathroom."

"It wasn't there, and I had to go bad."

"I'll get you one today." His voice softened as a grin lined his face. "You came out to watch the sun rise? Is it doing something today it doesn't usually do?" We laughed lightly. But he sat on the top step, his back against the porch beam, face set toward mixing colors in the sky. "That's the best thing about a day, and most people miss it most of their lives."

"I was going to sketch it." I pulled my pad and chalk bag out. Violet swirling in myriad blues and pastel pinks supplanted all questions and fears for moments that stretched into yellow-glazed orange. Silently, we looked to an ever brightening yellow slowly overtaking an orangy red glow in the center of the horizon. Pete's eyes feasted on the zillionth rising of the sun as though it would never happen again.

"What were you looking for?" I asked.

"Just wanted to make sure everything was all right. That, ah . . ." He trailed off.

"That there were no bombs like up by Goldsboro?"

"Bombs?" He tried to laugh it off, but I'd hit the nail on the head and could not join him. He turned away from the dawn to me. Our eyes locked. "You don't worry about that. You don't worry about that, hear?"

But after looking for a bomb in the truck, the tractor, and our car, my uncle who loved the sunrise did the final check by turning on the ignition. That's when they go off. I knew that from the movies.

"Why don't you come to New York with us? That's why Daddy came to New York."

He smiled and shook his head *no*. And I understood. It was *in* him, as Mommy would say, it was *in* him to be a freedom rider, and he couldn't outrun it if he tried. I thought about Hodges' and Miss Luella, and that made me happy and sad at the same time.

"Besides," he said, breaking a short but seemingly endless silence, "too many buildings. Hides that right there." He pointed to the sun, that had just stepped through soothing rings of color. Warm rays melted fears and emitted comfort. I flipped the page on my pad and began drawing Uncle Pete's shining profile in cinnamon browns and yellowy whites. I hummed the chant again. He picked it up. We sang softly with the birds.

> "But the Lord is in His holy temple;
> Let all the earth keep silence before Him.
> Keep silence. Keep silence.
> Keep silence before Him!"

From the kitchen the sound of clanking pots joined the new day.

"When are you getting married?" Daddy kidded Aunt Minnie Ruth during Easter Sunday dinner around Ma Pudnum's crowded kitchen table.

"Maybe soon, maybe later . . . maybe not."

"Better be soon, 'cause I tell you what, Sister—you ain't no spring chicken no more."

"You coming to my wedding?"

"Listen, when you get married, I'm gonna tell my customers to kiss my—"

"Watch it!" Mommy yelled, laughing.

"Butt—I got a wedding to go to! I got to see that for myself!"

Booby-trap bombs and Hodges' voices circled my head like a wicked halo, but everything was fun and gay for everyone else. I was ready to go home until Uncle Pete announced at Easter Sunday dinner that he was going to be a freedom rider instead of a tobacco picker the coming summer. No one smiled. There was no backslapping and high chests like when he told them he was going to college after graduation. Aunt Minnie Ruth opened her mouth to comment, and corn bread fell out. It was a sign, Aunt Willie Mae said. Aunt Christine let out a terrified "Lord, have mercy." But my heart did a silent jig.

Soon the badgering and advising started. Ma Pudnum told him to pray and let his conscience be his guide. Daddy told him to come to New York or get an M16. Aunt Bennie told him to ask God for grace to accept the way things were. Aunt Creola told him to join the army and get away from things. And Uncle Willie kept insisting things weren't so bad.

Mommy told him, whatever he did, finish school first. "I understand how you feel, Petey, but if you become a freedom rider, how are you going to pay for school in the fall?" she said carefully.

"I've been working two jobs this semester. With that plus my haircutting, I'll be able to go back." The crowded kitchen hushed. Miss Luella broke the stillness with an obvious imitation of her usual brashness.

"I personally don't give a damn—"

"Luella!"

" 'Bout eating next to no white folks," she continued, ignoring her husband's interruption. "And I sures don't want them fixin' me nothing to eat. They's nasty, I know, 'cause I clean their house every day!" She was rolling her eyes all over the place but looking no one in the eye. Hodges'. Her shame ricocheted and hit Craig and me at the same time. Our eyes scurried around the room searching for a place to hide before meeting just over the brim of a half-full pitcher of iced tea. Quickly we looked away, me to my plate; Craig, I don't know; my eyes were on my plate.

"Well, I can't say I have a burning desire to eat next to them, but I want to vote," Ma Pudnum said thoughtfully. "It don't make no kind of sense that the Negro school's new desks should be the white school's old ones! The tax man don't give me not nary a penny off my bill because I'm a Negro woman. I don't pay no hand-me-down taxes, so why should my children get hand-me-down books? But they can keep their hamburgers—that ain't no food nohow. I want to vote."

"But it's all the same." Uncle Pete was on fire. "It's about us being people. It's about our rights as human beings! We're human beings!" he said, jumping out of his seat.

"Boy, you must be foolish. Sit down." Miss Luella cast her eye askance at Pete. "Get yourself all worked up 'cause of what white folk think about you." Strutting, sassy, don't-give-a-damn Miss Luella. Where were you yesterday?

"Matter of fact, the less they think about you, the better off you'll be," Uncle Willie chimed in. "You might have some peace."

"I got news for you," Miss Luella continued. "You can do all the freedom working you want to do, white folk's going to do what white folk want to do, 'cause white folk's going to let them do it. Besides, I don't need no white folks' permission to be a human being. The good Lord took care of that right nicely many years ago, thank you."

"But they don't treat you like that, Miss Luella! You've

been buying from the Hodges' store for years, but when you go uptown with your green money, you have to wait until everybody white in the store is served, even some giggling girls who can't wipe themselves without getting their hands wet!''

I should have slapped those girls. I should have slapped those girls so hard . . . Warm salty blood eased over the side of my tongue, but I didn't stop biting my jaws, because if I did . . .

''Boy, don't be hollerin' at me! I ain't deaf! And if you're so worried 'bout somebody respecting me, you can start by doing it yourself!''

''What white folks thought about our humanity wouldn't matter one bit if they didn't have the power to shove it into our lives every day! But they do. In the stores, in the banks, in the courts, in the school, in the damn bathroom!'' Uncle Pete yelled and threw up his hands.

''Do it! Do it, do it, do it! *Do it!*'' I was screaming. And crying? And standing? Daddy and Craig, the only ones who had not stopped eating at Uncle Pete's announcement, put down their forks. ''Uncle Pete, I'm glad you're going to be a freedom worker this summer.''

''What happened to you, Sheryl?'' Daddy demanded.

''Yesterday when we went to Hodges', Ronnie wanted some water, but he couldn't reach the fountain—''

''Hodges' is a white fountain.'' Aunt Minnie Ruth shook her head.

''No, it was mostly green,'' Ronnie said sadly. ''And the water tasted funny. And the man yelled at us for drinking it.''

''He said *nigras* couldn't use their fountain. Then he

wiped it out *with ammonia*." Uncle Pete pulled me to his chest and rocked me back into my seat. I cried.

Daddy got up from the table. "Y'all finish eating and get your things together. We're going home." He walked out the kitchen with Mommy on his heels, pleading for one more day with her mother.

"Why didn't you say something to us?" Craig said.

"Something like what? That's the law here, right? I didn't know what to say. But I spit in that fountain before we left the store."

Grandma groaned. I messed up. Should have kept my mouth shut another day, just one more day, and Mommy wouldn't be about to cry now. Grandma wouldn't be groaning. Daddy wouldn't be cursing.

"Mama, when the law is in your hands, everything you do, right or wrong, is legal," Uncle Pete said. Miss Luella looked at him, then down into her plate of cooling food. He sighed and turned to her, placing an arm around her shoulder. "We can change that. I'll be doing voter registration this summer. You're gonna let me get you signed up, right, Mama Luella?" She did not smile, but clasped Uncle Pete's hands tightly in hers and pressed them against her lips.

Uncle Enoch finally said, "Petey, you're like Timothy in the Bible." He laid his hand on Pete. "God didn't give you a spirit of fear, but of power and love and of a sound mind."

Pete looked up into Uncle Enoch's eyes. "You know I'm still with you to work the farm. I'll fit the freedom work in around the farm."

"Do what you got to do." Uncle Enoch looked around

47

the room with eyes that dared anyone to speak. But the earlier utterings hung in the room like mist in morning air. Uncle Willie got up to leave, throwing up his hands and muttering that Uncle Pete was going to find himself dangling from a tree. They stood facing each other, looking like the same person locked in a time warp: Uncle Pete tall and straight as a pine, eyes hard as flexed biceps; Uncle Willie just as tall and stockier, but with shoulders sagging and body bent, forming a question mark like the one in his eyes.

Bubbly dishwater fizzled out to a doubly dead down South Sunday afternoon. We finished cleaning the kitchen early. I don't think Mommy was mad at me, but the only thing she said to me the whole while we worked the kitchen was, "Here, put this in that cupboard over there, baby." Maybe she was just tired. God knows she had done some fancy dancing to convince Daddy that there wasn't "an open filling station between here and Chesapeake at least." Now Daddy was napping with the swing vote on whether we'd stay for the county Easter Monday fish fry.

Mommy and Ma Pudnum talked quietly in the kitchen till Grandma nodded off midsentence. Mommy woke her and walked her to her bed, then went into the room with Daddy.

Siesta. But I wasn't sleepy. I walked around the edge of the front porch, still dressed in my church clothes. Down South had changed. No, it hadn't. Might as well take these clothes off. No place to go, and you couldn't go if there were.

Pete walked out the door just as I was going in. His eyes gleamed. "Want to go for a ride?"

"Yeah! One minute!" I skipped inside to the mirror over

the couch in the sitting room and patted my bangs down. *Better go on, stupid beauty, before Daddy wakes up and makes you stay here.* I grabbed my mostly empty pocketbook and rushed out the door. Pete and Craig waited in the pickup with the motor running. Craig got out, and I climbed into the middle.

"Where're we going?"

"Fishing."

"Fishing?" I touched my clothes.

"You're all right. Except for those shoes, but then I don't see how you walk in them anyway." Uncle Pete and Craig had come out of their jackets and thin ties, but they weren't dressed for it either. Fishing, yeah, right. I sat back and watched the dusty road.

All afternoon we went from town to town, country church to country church, door to door, fishing for people who were brave enough to register to vote. We were freedom riders for a day. Some churches seemed to have been waiting for us: "When can you come back?" Others—some polite, some not, all full of fear—asked us to go away and please not come back. "Go'ne now. We in the soul-saving business 'round here! We don't want no trouble! Go'ne now!"

We were lepers on the Negro front porches on the outskirts of Hendsonville. They shook their heads and walked away, gathering barefoot children. Barefoot on Easter Sunday. That was poor.

"See that house over there?" said the one old man who would speak to us, pointing to an empty leaning shack. A sharecropper with nine children used to live there until he was spotted talking with the freedom riders, he told us. "Hardworking man. Now his family's scattered. Tch, living from pillar to post."

I was waiting for him to say "Please don't start no trouble 'round here" when he asked us to his house up the road.

"Why aren't you afraid too?" I asked.

"Who said we're not?" His wife handed us cool glasses of sweet well water. "But we own this place, thank the Lord."

They brought us damp cloths for our sweaty faces and basins of water for our tired feet. They cut melons off of vines and offered us large juicy pieces to eat as they told us the stories of their lives. And yes, they finally said, they wanted to vote.

Black Hendsonville was really about eight miles from Hendsonville, which had no colored school. The nearest school for Negroes was more than thirty miles away, and a bus to take students there was not in the hamlet's budget. So, although the law said kids have to go to school at least until they turn sixteen, no Negro in Hendsonville did. Before registration could come to these backwoods, education had to move in. They would have to make a Freedom School here, Uncle Pete said.

"I can figure, and Mama can write and read, right, Mama?" The old man looked at his wife with the eyes of a best friend.

"Yes, yes, I can." She hurried into the small house, returning with a large Bible. She opened it and read slowly from Isaiah.

" 'How beautiful on the mountains are the feet of those who bring good news; who proclaim peace, who bring good tidings, who proclaim salvation, who say to Zion, "Your God reigns!" ' "

She closed the book and smiled. "My, y'all's feets is pretty today."

5 ◘◘◘◘◘◘◘◘◘◘◘◘◘◘◘◘◘

Easter Monday was a holiday, but the school buses rolled to the annual county fish fry. Meeting place was the schoolhouse; then we went down to the river for fresh catch and games. Craig and Ronnie would come later with the rest of the family, but I planned to take the school bus to be with Debra Jean. Another cousin who lived up the road would tell the driver to stop at Ma Pudnum's for me.

"Here comes the bus," I said, and started for the road.

Ma Pudnum squinted at the shiny yellow bus zooming up the road, using the back of her hand to block the blinding glow of the new-day sun. "Wait a minute." She shook her head. "No, that's the white bus." She went back to watering her coleus.

A white bus. I'd heard about them, but now, sure enough, here was one. I blinked and squinted. Before Saturday, I would have laughed to see how ridiculous grown folk could be. But Hodges' had taken the humor out of *white only* for me.

Ronnie stopped singing to look. "No, Ma Pudnum, that's not the white bus—that's the yellow bus," he said, and resumed singing his own song. Grandma smiled, but didn't explain that the yellow bus was for white children. Playful shouts and giggles floated from the windows of the shiny bus that didn't even slow down as it passed Ma Pudnum's house—sounds not unlike the ones from the school buses at home that were reserved for the elementary school kids. A white bus!

"Oh, oh, Sheryl, it didn't stop!" Ronnie said. For a second confusion covered his face, but he adjusted quickly. "That's okay—you can ride with us." He went back to his song.

I sat on the porch. "So that's the white bus? Does it do anything different from other buses?"

"Yeah," Ma Pudnum answered, "it works."

"They going to the fish fry too?"

"Um-hum. But on the other side of the river." She moved on to her geraniums and hot pink azaleas. Just as the white yellow bus reached the fork in the road by Clyde Dean's house, we heard a ruckus from the other direction. I turned toward the noise. Coming over the top of the hill was another yellow bus. But all the oil in Texas couldn't have made this one shine, rusty and corroded as it was. This one stopped.

"Go on." Ma Pudnam stopped her watering and looked at me. "That's the colored bus come for you."

We climbed through a back window of the long one-story brick schoolhouse. Of course, Debra's homeroom was at the end of the long corridor.

"What if the door's locked?" I whispered.

"It's open. I hope," she said. "Stay low. We'll catch it

if Miss Berry finds out we're in here.'' Debra opened the door just enough for us to slip in. There were six rows of old single desks that opened from the top, like I'd seen in old Lil' Rascals movies. I crawled behind Debra to the middle desk in the third row. She lifted it from the side and pulled out a blue oversize textbook held together with masking tape. Stamped inside the front cover was SALISBORO HIGH SCHOOL, followed by signatures and dates of the book's holders. On the opposite page was a Carter G. Woodson High School stamp.

"This used to be called Salisboro High School?''

"No, Salisboro is the white school," Debra Jean said, matter-of-factly. She pulled out a folded sheet of loose-leaf paper and eased the book back into the desk. We crawled back out the door, then raced down the hall, exiting through the window.

Debra Jean handed the barely legible, scrawled note to me.

Dear Debra Jean,

Everybody's talking about what a shame it is that you and Melvin Jenkins had to break up right before the fish fry. Everybody except for me, that is. I hope you are not too sad over it, because I am glad.

Look forward to talking with you Monday. I hope your mama lets you come.

Truly yours,
Michael Evans

"Ooh, who's Michael Evans?''

"And he's in the eleventh grade. He lives across the creek." Debra Jean smiled a little smile.

"Is Melvin Jenkins here?"

"Uh-huh, but I won't have to show you who he is." Debra Jean refolded the note. "You'll know before the day's over, believe me."

"Do you still kind of like him?"

"Nope. Not even a little bit. He asked this other girl to be his girlfriend while he was supposed to be being my boyfriend. Not only that, Sheryl, but the girl he asked is my second cousin on my daddy's side. How was I not supposed to find out? He used to be nice before somebody told him that he was cute. Now his head's so big, it's done damaged his brain." I threw my head back and laughed, sucking in giant gulps of country air scented with the green aroma of dew-moistened grass.

We walked over to a swing made from a piece of wood and rope hanging from a huge oak tree in front of the schoolhouse. I sat thinking about this strange place. Debra Jean pushed.

How in the world did one flat T-shaped building hold all of Salisboro's first through twelfth graders? Well, not all, only the Negro ones. Better question yet, why in the world would one flat T-shaped building hold all Salisboro's Negro first through twelfth graders? The town had bigger new elementary and high schools—schools that we had to pass to reach this one. Salisboro was beautiful, but strange. At home, there weren't many white kids at school either, but then, there weren't many white families around there, except for the Hasidic Jews over by Eastern Parkway, and they went to their own schools. But that wasn't all that was strange about this school. New textbooks were old, and the desks were antiques. It was a Jim Crow school.

"Debra—"

I was going to ask her how she could stand seeing Jim Crow every day of the week when another bus pulled up and the answer walked out.

Debra Jean kept pushing the swing, but whispered, "There he is, Sheryl."

His bus must have been the last one scheduled to arrive, because no sooner had he gotten off than a cowbell sounded. (That's right, a cowbell.) Hundreds of kids on the ground quickly went to designated class areas. High schoolers gathered in front of their school wing and grade schoolers by theirs. In no time we were filing back onto buses. They rolled down a two-lane highway that hugged the river and crossed the worn bridge. The heavy rains of the last few nights had forced the creek up to bridge level. We rode past trees with their trunks high in the river, fighting against its current.

A crowd had already gathered at the river by the time we reached the picnic ground. Women tended fires and mixed hush-puppy batter, intermittently fanning away flies hovering around pots of cooked collard greens. Men on the water drew in nets of jumping fish to the banks. Others cleaned batches caught earlier. It all smelled so good!

Games immediately began to form all over the open field. Away from the cooking, I sat with Debra Jean and her friends on a large tree stump next to a patch of wild honeysuckle. Debra Jean picked two. She put the nectar from one behind each ear and sucked the other. We could join in the field games and competitions later.

Forget Jim Crow. This was a good day.

An older boy nearby toyed with a football. Before the ball even left his hands, I knew it was en route to my head. We weren't in the line of play, but I knew it was going to hit me. I felt it. And, sure enough, somewhere between Mississippi five and Mississippi six, it landed upside my head. Even I had to laugh. The guy who threw it ran across the field and caught me about a minute after the hit, even though I wasn't falling.

"Are you all right?" the guy said.

"Yeah."

"Sure? Wouldn't want to damage a thing on you," he said, still holding my shoulders. I wiggled free, then glanced into Debra Jean's smirking eyes.

"No, I'm fine."

"You look it."

"I know it." I heard a fly girl say that to Craig once. Been waiting since then to be able to use that line.

He smiled pretty, winked, and ran back to the game. I looked at Debra Jean. "Melvin," we said together, and fell out laughing.

By midafternoon tall glasses of iced tea could do nothing about a too-hot sun. In the cool of the willow was the place to be. Seniors, juniors, sophomores, and freshmen formed their own clusters under the row of trees by the side of the river and tuned small transistor radios to the same soul station out of Charlotte. I Mashed Potatoes with a slew of boys, including Melvin. Some dances we all knew, but they had some wild local ones named after animals, like the Dog, the Chicken, and, my favorite, the Turtle. Learning that one was fun, but it could sure wear a neck and shoulders out! Craig was a hit with the girls at Woodson High. They loved the way he talked, walked, danced. And if all of that wasn't enough, he was kin to Uncle Pete.

The senior girls called out "Hey, Pete!" letting the world know they knew the graduate. The junior girls waved and wistfully dreamed of the next year, when they'd be seniors and chummy with graduates returning from big northern cities, or the army, or college. Pete stood talking to a group of the older kids when Marvin Gaye began crooning out "Hitchhike" over the airwaves. One of the senior girls playfully caught Pete's arm and moved him away from the group to a clear space for dancing.

"You can talk later, Peter Lamont James! Right now, you and I are going to tear up this grass!" He lifted his hands in surrender and turned to face his partner. She smiled right into his eyes. He winked.

His boogaloo was so cool.

Daddy skipped the fish fry to sleep. And when we returned, our bags were in the car, which was gassed up and ready to make the journey north. We washed and kissed good-bye.

"Y'all don't let it be so long 'fore y'all come back. Okay, Robert?" Ma Pudnum hugged Daddy.

"Tell you what, Mama, I'm gonna come and get you to stay with us for a while when I go on vacation this summer." Daddy stroked Ma Pudnum's cheek.

"Me up there? With all those people? Noooo-mmmmaybe." We laughed.

"You come too," I told Uncle Pete. He brushed my bangs down in three quick swipes with his hands, imitating my all-day habit. He didn't know it, but I was praying when we hugged tight.

We piled into the our brown Bonneville.

Virginia, Maryland, Delaware, New Jersey—then around midnight that same Easter Monday night, we were back in Brooklyn getting ready for school the next day.

6 ◻◻◻◻◻◻◻◻◻◻◻◻◻◻◻

Jim Crow was miles away from Junior High School 210 in Brooklyn, but its putrid odor steeped my memory like a marinade. I smelled it all through my first day back at school. I'd be diagramming English sentences or conjugating Spanish verbs, and its stench would just rise like conjured haints. I tried to breathe it out, think it away, only to smell it again in an hour or so. *Nigras.*

It wasn't a weightless fume either; it was heavy and packed with images and groanings words could not utter: *Nigras* and the white bus, hot fences and Hendsonville, bombs in the night. It made me tired, made me walk slow and close my eyes, shut my mind off and sleep, and sleep, and sleep. And for lunch I did just that—went to the nurse's office and slept for an hour.

Needless to say, my first day back at school in Brooklyn went s-l-o-w-l-y. Hands downs, the best part of this day was when it was over and I met my friends in front of the school to walk home.

Pamela and I were in the same class, but she was Ackerson and tall and I was Williams and short. So whether a teacher assigned seats by alphabetical order or height, we were never near each other. Her twin, Patrice, was in another ninth grade homeroom, as teachers made a point of not putting them in the same class. Both were tall and thin, with opal-smooth black skin and friendly voices that pranced around high C. At first glance there's no way to tell them apart. I couldn't tell them apart either, till around third grade when their personalities took over, and they started looking more like them than each other. Now they were my best friends.

"Hi, twins!"

"Hi, Sheryl," they said as we fell in step down Prospect Place.

"How was the trip?" Patrice asked.

"It was good, I guess—most of the time."

"Your grandmother get an indoor bathroom yet?"

"Nope."

"Ugh—I don't understand. Why would anybody build a bathroom outside of a house?" she said.

"It's not like a real bathroom," I tried to explain. "There's no sink or bathtub or mirror or flushable toilet in an outhouse. It's just a small wood hut with a bench inside that has two circles cut out. You hold your breath, sit over the circles, and do what you have to do."

"What happens after you go?"

"What do mean, 'What happens?' " I asked.

"Where does the stuff go?"

"It doesn't go anywhere. It sits and stinks. That's why they put it outside."

One twin started scratching. That was Pamela. Nasty things made her itch.

"But that wasn't the funkiest part of the trip. Anybody ever call you a *nigra*?" I was about three feet ahead of them before I realized the twins had frozen, Pat with her one hand free of books on her hip and Pam with her head down and eyes glaring up at me.

"Somebody called you a nigger, Sheryl?" Pam asked indignantly.

"No, but a man called me a nigra."

"Well, I hope that you slapped him, because *nigra* is *nigger* with a southern accent," Pat said in angry staccato.

I told the twins about Miss Luella's glove purchase and Carter G. Woodson High School, about Debra Jean's books and Ma Pudnum's land. Pat assured me that I had shown the man in the store by spitting in the fountain, but I knew better. If I'd gone back to Hodges' that second, the spit would be gone, but I still wouldn't be allowed to drink from that fountain. Uncle Pete's freedom plans for the summer made more sense.

The only thing that saved the twins from joining me in a deepening blue funk was George Pitts and Parker Allen, who were in front of us vying for the latest girl in school to get their attention. This one was an import—she was from the Dominican Republic, somebody said. How they always ended up interested in the same girl at the same time was beyond me. I don't think they ever liked any girl half as much as they liked ranking each other out.

"You were so ugly when you were born, the doctor had to slap the nurse to stop her from laughing!" George yelled.

That was tired, which was normal for them. Then Parker started spinning around and singing in falsetto about how fine this new girl was, like he was a Miracle or something.

"What are these fools doing?" Pat said, interrupting my trip story to point to a sight ahead. "Should we intervene?"

"Why? It's a free country. They can act like jackasses on a street corner if they want to," Pam said.

By the end of the second block, where George and Parker had to turn off for their homes, they were imitating James Brown. George's thick legs shocked everyone when they slid into a scissor split and up again with ease. The whole sidewalk clapped and cheered. Even fat Mr. Carroll, the candy store man, whistled from his window. Simpering, Parker squeezed his eyes and put his head down, listening to sidewalk taunts and knowing that George's act would be a hard one to match.

"Hey, Parker, your mama, she callin' you, man!"

"Cry, cry, cry, ohoo, your blues away!" Patrice sang loudly.

Then, giving him a rank concealed as a kindness, the new girl smiled and spoke sweetly to Parker in a lilting Spanish accent. " 'You don' hav' to if you *can't*.' "

Now the poor boy *had* to do it.

Claps rose from the small crowd as Parker prepared for the feat. Down, down, slowly, slowly (well, he did have sneakers on). With about a foot left, the front heel of Parker's right sneaker slipped into some spit or some something, and he lost control. In that second, not only did his legs split, but so did his pants. We laughed the rest of the way home.

* * *

That night at dinner our family shared the day's stories from work and school over the sound of the evening TV news, as usual. But for one report Daddy hushed us. On the screen was a policeman in dark mirror shades and a light helmet knocking a young Negro woman to the ground. When she tried to get up, he hit her with his nightstick. Her knees came up to her face, her arms covering her head. He grabbed her by the back of the shirt collar and dragged her up the street, and the blouse began choking her. She unfolded, gasping for air, and the buttons popped off, exposing a white bra for a fraction of a second. The camera quickly switched to a young Negro man with blood streaming down his face trying to get his leg out of a vicious German shepherd's mouth. A policeman calmly held the dog by a leash, making no effort to pull it off. They cut to another town, this one in North Carolina. Negro students sat at a food counter waiting to be served. A customer came up behind one and dumped ketchup on the man's head. Police came and ushered the students out to paddy wagons. *The students* were charged with disturbing the peace, a newscaster said before the station cut to a toothpaste commercial.

I twirled spaghetti on my fork and thought about the freedom workers. And knew that somewhere out there in all that hate was Uncle Pete.

7 ◧◩◧◩◧◩◧◩◧◩◧◩◧◩◧◩◩

Spring teased Brooklyn the next day with temperatures in the high sixties and a shining sun that reminded me of summer to come, and, Lord, what it held for Uncle Pete and his freedom workers. Snarling dogs and sheriffs. But could it hold freedom too? Would it—

"Am I disturbing you, She-ryl?" Mr. Miller's voice boomed down my neck, making me jump. My pen and thoughts flew somewhere over the next desk. He stood over my shoulder and stared down at the dogs and hands clutching jail bars that crowded my notes on the Louisiana Purchase. "Would you like for me to get you some paints and an easel too?"

There was snickering from the front of the classroom. I kept my eyes on my paper and shook my head no.

"I didn't hear you!"

This would never happen to a fly girl.

The end-of-period bell rang before he could really dig in.

I kept my eyes on my desk, closing my books and putting them away, while the rest of the kids shuffled out into the noisy lunchtime hallway. The room cleared quickly. Even Mr. Miller was gone by the time I got up to leave.

Pam waited at the back door, shaking her head. "Forget about him. Sheryl, he hates everybody."

"Why couldn't he just ask me a question about the Louisiana Purchase? I read the homework. How can somebody wake up that mean *every day*! Oops!" Darin Fogey, who sits next to me, was leaning on the wall outside of the classroom, holding out my pen. I almost walked right into him.

"He sleeps with the devil," he said, and stuck my pen in my jacket pocket.

We were still laughing when we met Pat, George, Parker, Eddie, and the new girl outside. With light jackets draped over our shoulders and thick sweaters tied about our hips, we strolled to Lincoln Terrace Park to eat bag lunches and get in a few games of handball. A warm wind whished away thoughts of Mr. Miller, leaving the vivid picture of Uncle Pete and those dogs that got me in trouble in the first place.

"Who has a ball?" Pat yelled. The boys looked at one another, but no one said a word. Pat rolled her eyes and muttered, "How're we going to play handball without a ball?" She marched into the store. We followed.

My friends roamed the store, picking up potato chips, gum, soda. I was standing at the door, checking my empty pockets for money I knew wasn't there, when I saw the headline.

NEGROES STOP BUSINESS IN BIRMINGHAM—*story on page 3*.

I stuffed my lunchbag under my arm, picked up the paper, and turned to the story. A large photo of chanting students

64

in police wagons was next to the story. For a second, just a second, Uncle Pete and those dogs replaced it.

"Hey, this ain't the library! I don't rent papers—I sell them. Buy that paper or put it down!"

Pppsh! Twice in one afternoon! What is this! I glanced up a little. Thank God nobody was paying attention. The shopkeeper was yelling, but there was too much other noise in the store.

"And straighten it back out. The only thing a used paper is good for is—"

"Here's for the paper." Darin put a dime on the counter.

The shopkeeper took it and started yelling at everybody else. "Hey! Cut out that noise back there! This ain't no playground!"

"Not your day, huh, Sheryl?" Darin said.

I mumbled thanks and slid out of the door, looking back into the paper.

"What are you reading anyway?"

I pointed to the article with my chin. Crumbs from Darin Fogey's chips dropped over my shoulder onto page 3. I blew them away and read aloud.

"Birmingham, Alabama: Negroes continued protesting against segregation despite a county court injunction prohibiting such action."

"Man, I saw that on TV last night!" Darin stepped back to demonstrate. "This Negro man was trying to get away from this police dog—a big German shepherd chewing his leg off, man. Then the cop came over, took his stick, and went *whop!* right upside the man's head. Blood came gushing—"

"You should have got the Spalding, twin!" George waved his hand.

"*You* should have got the Spalding. I like Pinksy Pinkers!" Pat retorted.

"You think he's alive?" I asked.

"Huh?" Darin looked at me, but all I could see was Uncle Pete. "The man that got beat? I guess. I don't know. Yeah, he's alive. Got a hellified headache, though."

Pam came and peeked over our shoulders to see what we were doing. Pat joined her sister, and the boys, not tired of harassing her, came too. I continued reading aloud.

"Dr. Martin Luther King, Jr., said he and other local ministers will lead a protest tomorrow.

'I am prepared to go to jail and stay as long as necessary,' he said."

By the end of the article, we had reached the park and settled on a bench not far from the handball court under the budding trees. We had meant to eat quickly, then get a few games in before going back to class, but the day's news changed those plans.

"Man, they're crazy!" Darin said, popping the last bit of his sandwich into his mouth. He clapped the crumbs out of his hands. "I'm telling you, I saw them on TV last night. After the police finished beating them up, they sicced German shepherds on them! And they still wouldn't hit back!"

"That's called nonviolent resistance, civil disobedience," Pat said.

"That's called stupid!" George said before gulping the last of his grape soda.

"Sheryl's uncle's there, right Sheryl?" Pam said.

"Not in Birmingham. He's working in our hometown, Salisboro, North Carolina."

"I never saw anything on TV from anyplace called Salisboro," George said.

"So, just because you didn't see something on TV doesn't mean it didn't happen, George," Pat said.

"I didn't say it didn't happen! I just said I didn't see it. That's why you need to mind your business, twin."

"How do you know what I need to do and you don't even know who I am? You—"

"It's happening all over the South, not just Birmingham. The freedom riders are all over. And my uncle's one."

"They're crazy to let anybody beat up on them like that," George said.

I tried to explain. "No, it's like this, George—"

"No, it's like this!" George pointed to an article in the lower left corner of the page.

"Real men don't put their children on the firing line," said Eastern Muslim leader Malcolm X.

Negro bystanders, angered by attacks on student protesters, hurled rocks at police, a departure from Dr. King's doctrine of nonviolence.

"Good," George said. "At least somebody down there has sense enough to fight back."

"Well, why don't they all fight back?" Darin asked.

That was a good question that I really didn't know the answer to, but I told them what I'd heard. "My uncle said Jim Crow—that's what they call laws against Negroes down there—has more guns and people to use them than we do. But they're going to help it destroy itself by just standing up to it and letting it show the world how evil it is."

"I think they think that if they fought back, they'd get beat up," Pamela said, and erased any doubt George could have had about which twin she was. Pam would do anything to avoid fighting, and when she couldn't, Pat did it for her. But this latest dodge was much, even for Pam. We just looked at her like she was crazy. The whole world knew the freedom workers were getting beat up every day anyway.

Pat rolled her eyes from her sister to George. "No, it's because an Indian man named Mohandas—"

"Ma-who?" George laughed.

"Gandhi," Pat said harshly, flashing her eyes at George for interrupting, "used it to free his people."

"Free them from what?" George asked.

"You mean *who*—the British," Pat said.

"In England?"

"No, in India. I said he was Indian!"

"You said they had to get free of the British!"

"They did!"

"In India?"

"Oh, Lord."

"What were the English doing in India?"

"Bothering the Indians, George, bothering the Indians!" Pat yelled. "Haven't you ever heard anybody say 'The sun never sets on the British Empire'?"

"No," George said, getting pissed, "I don't know anybody but you that goes around talking about the British Empire."

"Well, England owned so many other countries all over

the world that when a day ended in one of them, it was just beginning in another. My grandfather told me. He's from Barbados, and England still owns his country.''

"Look, anybody that got the sense they were born with knows you don't go wolfin' for a fight if you're outnumbered,'' Parker said. "In so many words, that's what Sheryl's uncle told her.''

"George, all that Pat's talking doesn't have anything to do with Alabama,'' Darin said.

"It has to do with Alabama because they're using that Indian's strategy to fight without guns.'' Patrice tried to calm down.

"It's probably not his advice they're taking, but Jesus', them being preachers and all,'' Parker said. "You know how the Bible says if somebody hits you on your left cheek, you're supposed to show them your right one so they whop that one too.''

"No, it's Gandhi,'' Pat assured us. "I read it in the newspaper.''

"It could still be Jesus. 'Just because you didn't see it in the newspaper don't mean it didn't happen'!'' George mocked the twin's earlier rank on him.

"So, Sheryl,'' Darin said, "you mean your uncle is letting them beat him up? What's the matter with him? I'm not that scared of anybody.''

"Right!'' George slapped him five. "They might take me out, but I won't be by myself.''

"No, he's not afraid,'' I said slowly, only half-believing it but sure I wasn't lying, remembering the bomb check.

"Dr. King said the freedom workers just aren't going to lower themselves to those people's level of hate,'' Pat said.

"Oh, shoot!" George was disgusted. "It's a shame to protect yourself, but not a shame to get your butt kicked on national television? You must be Pam."

"What's that supposed to mean?" Pat asked.

"Guess, Pamela."

"I'm Pat."

George laughed. "Uh-uh, you can't be Pat. You can't be Volcano Mouth! Featherweight champion of Junior High Two-Ten and—"

"Your mother's the—"

"Hey!" Suddenly their joking turned into real anger. "Don't even start that. Don't talk about my mother. I'm not nonviolent!" George glared at Pat, then added, "And neither are you."

In one horrifying snort, George sucked up a glob of spit into his mouth. We'd all seen the freedom riders spit on on TV. Now George moved toward Pat. She stiffened, jumped off the railing where she sat, and moved toward George.

"Boy, I'll knock you into next week."

George's spit hit the sidewalk with a loud splat, away from Pat and anyone else. "Told you," he said.

We breathed.

Pam changed the subject. "What time is it?"

"Oh, shoot, it's one-thirty!" Parker answered.

We took off out of the park. We were going to be late for class.

With birds chirping and a blinding sun heating an already stuffy classroom, it was hard enough to concentrate in English that afternoon without Darin's bored notes. But since I couldn't focus anyway, they were welcome. He'd made captain of the softball team, he wrote. I congratulated him in capital letters surrounded by stars and exclamation points. He returned modest thanks in pretty caps and small cursive. I complimented his handwriting. He pointed to the thanks note again. He was sort of nervous, with the first game coming up Saturday, he said. Darin didn't have anything to worry about. The neighborhood softball star since I'd met him in the fifth grade, he was the only logical choice for captain, and I told him so. He looked at me sort of surprised. I gave him a you-know-it's-the-truth-so-why-are-you-looking-at-me-like-that face. He smiled and changed the subject.

Was there anything that we could do to help my uncle and the other freedom workers this summer, he asked, half-cursive, half-print, both pretty. I drew a question mark. Short of going down there, which I knew I couldn't, I didn't know. But I guessed they could always use money—bail money, supplies money, living money, escape money, and money to go back to school with. Figures they'd need the one thing he didn't have, he wrote. Right! I wrote. We could get money, he wrote, by selling candy or something. We'd have to buy the stuff first. Let's keep thinking about it, I wrote, signing off, cued by the sound of classroom movement that it was near dismissal time. Wait, he wrote, why don't you bring your little brother to the game Saturday at Albany Avenue Park? Ronnie would like that, I wrote. I'll try. And the bell rang.

Outside George and Parker resumed their quest for the new girl. In the course of our conversation, she declared in a thick accent that she was not Negro, but "Domeenican." We thought she was putting on airs.

"No. That's your country. What are *you*?" Darin asked. We looked at each other out of the corners of our eyes.

"No. My country is the Dominican Republic. *I* am Dominican."

Darin slapped his forehead.

"Is that something like Puerto Rican?" Pamela asked diplomatically.

"No. Both are Spanish-speaking countries, but we do different because different countries."

"Like what?"

"Like food a' music. Some same, but different," she said, smiling. When we still looked blank, she demonstrated. "See, Puerto Ricans dance this way." With one arm raised above her head, she whirled herself around to her left, then stopped. "We dance this way." She switched the arm she raised and whirled to the right. We laughed, and so did she. She wasn't putting on airs.

We looked at her brown arms. Her skin was light, but not white. I'd seen plenty of Negroes with even lighter skin.

"So why's your hair like this?" Darin touched the nappy edges of her long but woolly dark brown hair. She scrunched up her face like he'd said the dumbest thing she'd ever heard.

"The same reason as yours!" She touched his tight kinks but politely refrained from adding "stupid!"

"My hair's like this because my ancestors came from Africa!"

"So, mine too!"

"Oh," Darin said, sounding as stupid as we all felt and must have looked. But he rebounded quick. "So why didn't you say so in the first place?"

"Because you did not ask in the second place!" she yelled back.

"See, when you said you were Dominican, we thought you meant you were white," I explained. Now she thought we were *all* stone fools.

"White! I'm not white," she said, holding her arm up next to Darin's.

George laughed and pushed her arm down. "Nobody's as black as Darin."

Darin gave his usual answer: "Blacker the berry, the sweeter the juice," and took his arm back.

"Then you must be a raaaspberry, because you are *bl—ack*!" the girl said.

George and Parker howled. Even Darin had to laugh at that one.

No, she wasn't putting on airs. Maybe back where she came from, it mattered more that she was there than she was black. Well, she's here now.

We finally got to Utica Avenue and split off to our homes. The twins took a bus to their grandmother's. Darin and I walked up St. John's Place. He was going to work at his father's Laundromat. I was going home. We walked in silence until we approached the sidewalk fruit market.

"Darin, have you ever tasted a raspberry?"

"Huh?"

"Look!" I pointed to the sign in the fruit stand advertising raspberries for thirty cents a pound.

"I have fifteen cents. Let's get half a pound." He dug into his pockets for the change and came out with an extra quarter. "Let's get a pound."

We rinsed off the bumpy black fruit under water dripping from a broken fire hydrant. Darin bit into a fat berry, squirting purple juice down his white shirt. I popped one in my mouth whole and bit slowly. For about ten minutes our silent bliss was interrupted only by a few *hmm*s and the rumpling of the paper bag emptying rapidly. While I chewed the last berry, Darin belched and smiled, revealing berry-stained lips, teeth, and tongue.

"Maybe I am a raspberry."

8 🔲🔲🔲🔲🔲🔲🔲🔲🔲🔲🔲🔲🔲🔲🔲🔲

On Saturdays the Laundromat is pack jammed. If you don't get there early, you could get stuck in that place all day. So I sorted clothes on Friday night and met Darin and his father at eight in the morning as they opened the gates of Fogey Wash and Dry.

Today the wash took three machines: one for whites, one for coloreds, and one for Craig's football mess. The night before, I'd argued with Mommy about my having to wash Craig's filthy stuff, and she'd exploded: "Look, miss, don't give me word for word! You're washing the clothes. You're washing *all* of the clothes, and I don't want to hear any more about it! Do you understand?" Mommy was edgy these days. Telephone contact with Ma Pudnum and Aunt Minnie Ruth kept us abreast of the danger Uncle Pete walked in, and that reality had taken the humor out of a lot of things for Mommy.

It was a reality that was hard to get away from. I'd be

walking down the street, minding my own business, and inadvertently I'd hear about the latest student protester arrests and injuries from neighborhood shoppers squeezing tomatoes at outdoor vegetable stands. And every day I watched TV news and read papers filled with things I hated but needed to know because everyone's knowing was the freedom workers' only protection. If the police and white citizen councils beat and jailed freedom workers with the whole world watching, what would they do in secret? Just kill them all and be done with it, that's what.

The other side of that story I saw etched in the faces of the freedom workers, young and old—hard-pressed but not crushed, perplexed but not despairing, persecuted but not abandoned, struck down but not destroyed. In facing the peril, they had gained something that could never be given or taken away by human hands. And I wondered what that felt like.

By a quarter after eight, all the clothes had begun the twenty-minute wash cycle. Going home didn't make sense, so I sat and sketched, thinking about marching and land surveys.

"Monkeys."

"Huh?"

"You drew the see-no-evil, hear-no-evil, speak-no-evil monkeys." Darin folded a shirt and examined the sketch over my shoulder. "You do a good monkey."

"Oh, I'm just drawing." My clothes stopped. I put them in two dryers and returned to find Darin leafing through my pad. "Sheryl, you're even better than I thought."

"Hum, thanks. That's my grandmother's house in North Carolina." He nodded and turned pages: kids playing handball against the side of a building, a car leaving a dusty trail up a country road, men cleaning fish by a river, the sun rising on Uncle Pete. He gave the book back, looking all funny, and waited on a man who wanted his small bag of laundry by six. When the man left, Darin emptied the small bag into a machine, then resumed folding clothes.

"Is that what you're going to do when you get grown—draw and be an artist?"

"Grow up? Please, I don't even want to think about it."

"Why not? Think about it or not, you're gonna do it." Darin climbed on top of a front-loading machine and turned on the radio sitting on the shelf above it.

"I don't like to think about it because . . . I'm just okay, you know. No, you don't know." He fixed the dial on the rhythm and blues station, then jumped down.

"What do you mean?" I shook my head and waved my hand for him to forget it and went back to sketching. People don't understand everything. You show them a secret place, and they look at you like you're crazy or, worse, give an understanding nod with eyes that reflect another time zone. Makes you feel alone. Darin stopped folding and sat down next to me. "No, Sheryl, come on. What do you mean?"

"When I think about being grown, I see long hot summer days with everyone on vacation, except me. Me and the empty block and a long day to fill.

"See, now you're the best in softball, the best in math, you make the best jokes, when you want to. I'm just okay—in everything. In all my subjects at school, except math maybe—I'm not even too okay in that, but everything else . . . I even look just okay. How in the world does a just-okay somebody grow up to a life that's not a long hot summer day with everybody on vacation, except for her?"

"I never thought of you as just okay, Sheryl. I sit next

to you in most our classes. Your grades in everything are . . . are . . .''

"Okay!'' we said together, and laughed.

"But dig it, Sheryl, you call that 'just okay'—I call that *balanced*. Yeah, I'm good in math. But I stink in English and I don't know what I'd do if I didn't sit next to you in social studies.''

"That's just because you don't care about those two subjects.''

"You're right.''

"Darin, you're great in stuff. And I'm not.''

"What!'' Darin grabbed my sketch pad out of my hand. "Look at this, and this, and this!'' he said while turning the pages of my sketchbook. "You're great in drawing, Sheryl! Are you blind?''

"Drawing? How do you make a living drawing? Tch, I like to eat too much for that.''

"People use pictures, Sheryl! The newspapers are full of them every day!'' Darin was flabbergasted. He ran to the back of the Laundromat and returned with an old newspaper. He opened to the pages and pages and pages of sketches of people modeling sale clothes and cars and household appliances and houses and, and, and . . .

"Sheryl, *somebody's* drawing these things. Might as well be you.''

He held the newspaper and I my sketchbook, both of us turning pages slowly, comparing the two. My sketches were as good as those in the paper, even better than some. Amazing. I didn't even know my own hands.

I got my clothes out the dryers, and folded them, and imagined. By nine-thirty I was going home.

"See you at the game, Darin.''

"Yeah?"

"Yeah."

"See you at the game." He held the door open while I pushed out my shopping cart full of clothes. "Oh, and by the way," he said before I went out myself, "you look a lot better than 'just okay.' What do you say to that?"

I bit my smiling lip and left.

9 🞑🞑🞑🞑🞑🞑🞑🞑🞑🞑🞑🞑🞑🞑🞑🞑

A few days later I heard from Debra Jean.

May 7, 1963

Dear Sheryl,

We saw Ma Pudnum's land get marked off on Saturday, and girl, it was better than a movie!

The surveyor came on Wednesday to walk out the deed. Clyde Dean came out with his shotgun and told the surveyor to get off his land. The surveyor made a beeline for his truck. Said he couldn't work under the circumstances! Ma Pudnum tried to talk to that mule Clyde Dean, but that was useless. Petey was over in Hendsonville working at the Freedom School they've started there (that's another story). But when he got back, he called and made another appointment with the surveyor for Saturday.

Ten o'clock Saturday morning, the surveyor drove up with a

fishing rod sticking out his back window. He was so sure he wasn't going to be doing any work! Clyde Dean and a few of his friends came out with shotguns and told the surveyor fish were really jumping up by Belltown! They were getting into catfish recipes when a shot rang out from Ma Pudnum's front door followed by Uncle Enoch, Petey, and some other folk from around here—all with rifles over their shoulders!

Petey yelled, "Get off our land, Clyde Dean!"

"And do it now!" Another voice and shot rang out, this one from the woods behind Clyde Dean and his posse. It was my mama! They exchanged a few words about whose land it was, but Clyde Dean's crew moved to let the surveyor do his job.

What a sight!

Next week the surveyor will give Ma Pudnum a map of her land.

Well, I knew you'd want to hear what happened! Kiss everybody for me, especially my little Pooh bear, Ronnie!

Love, your cousin,
Debra Jean

10 □□□□□□□□□□□□□□□

Aunt Emma could work a song, a red dress, and an offering. Daddy's sister did all three on Sunday, pointing the way to how we could help the freedom riders.

All of us in the junior choir had finished singing, and Aunt Emma and the other trustees were counting the offering. Our musician filled the silence with a heavily improvised hymn. We passed out candy and whispered until she played her two special loud chords, which we knew meant *shut up*. We temporarily abandoned conversations for private thoughts.

This sanctuary always reminded me of Noah's ark turned sideways. It was wide but short, with a high ceiling arched lengthwise. The stuccoed walls were painted in flat white and lined with mahogany wood trim that led to thick wood beams bending across the ceiling and separating six eight-foot skylight windows that bathed us in sun. There were eight long, arched windows in the balcony and eight more on ground level. I could see hay up there and birds, two of each kind, flying crisscross from one window to another— a pair of peacocks, in all of their fall-colored glory, perched on the banister, or two screeching South American macaws setting up on the windowpane. In back of the choir loft was a naked brick wall. It used to be a regular plastered wall, but hurricane rains had leaked through two falls ago and destroyed it. After the roof leak was fixed, the wall plaster was knocked out, and we discovered beautiful bare brick. Its warmth and texture belonged in our church. The church sexton made a simple cross from tree branches that had fallen during the storm. It hung, gnarled, unpolished, and unsanded, on that wall.

I could see hay there too, and was fixing to when the trustees' financial report told me where we could get money for the freedom riders. "We want to thank you, if there be no mistakes, for two hundred dollars for the guest speaker and three hundred fifty dollars for the church," one said.

Five hundred fifty dollars! And two hundred of that for a stranger!

Something inside said, "Enlist your Aunt Emma." But to do what?

Aunt Emma was decked out in red. On special request, she had sung a solo to honor the return of one of the church's convalescent Mothers. She marked the occasion with red shoes, red pocketbook, and red dress gloves. Red lipstick decorated her full mouth, and a feather-trimmed red skull hat nuzzled just over her right eye. A form-fitting red dress with matching jacket (also trimmed in feathers) neatly held her round hips. Daddy winced. I just wanted to be Aunt Emma. She turned up her nose at her brother and kissed

Mommy and me. We laughed. Daddy's eyes asked his brother-in-law, "Can't you do anything about this?" Uncle Walter shrugged. They laughed. Aunt Emma worked with her husband in their funeral parlor all week, and so insisted on dressing like a tropical isle on Sundays. Church elbows nudged and heads turned from every direction, but there was nothing to be said other than Emma Monroe looked good. She knew it too and sashayed all the way to our house for dinner.

"I'm glad we live up here and not down there." I passed Aunt Emma hot candied yams, recounting the trip for her. "You should have heard the way that Hodges' woman talked to Miss Luella! Like she was a kid!"

"Hmm, I've already heard and seen more of that kind of mess than I want to remember," Aunt Emma said, shaking her head while filling her fork with collards.

"But don't kid yourself," Daddy interjected. "These northern white folks ain't crazy about us either. They're just more sneaky about it."

"Please, I don't need white folks to be crazy about me. I have a good husband, family, and friends for that," Aunt Emma said, and put down her fork. "As for being sneaky, you can tell the ones that don't like you because they screw you up every chance they get. What do you expect, a thief to come up to you and say, 'Hey, Robert, I just stole your car'? No, they're not being sneaky, they're trying to be civilized, and that's the way I like it."

Civilized. Now, that's interesting. But how could it ever be civilized to steal somebody's car? I kept my thoughts to myself, though. I had to figure out just what it was I wanted Aunt Emma to help with.

"After I got out of the army, I worked in a steel mill in Gary, Indiana," Daddy said, contesting Aunt Emma with his own story. "Every week God sent, the white owners talked of closing the plant and layoffs. We'd take pay cuts, work longer hours so that we could have a job. Then come to find out they were expanding the plant, but still crying broke every week!" Daddy waved his hand in disgust. "How can a man think about having a family when he's constantly wondering if he's getting fired, if he'll get re-hired, if he'll be able to make a decent living?

"I quit that job and went to barber college on my GI bill."

I'd heard that story a million times. That one and how Daddy loved the rain when he was a boy because the only time he got to school was when he couldn't work in the field. I'd heard it all before. But after down South this time, it was different. Usually Daddy would start his stories and Craig and I would look at each other like, "Here we go again." (We had sense enough not to laugh.) But this time, we didn't. We had seen enough.

Uncle Walter, nodding his head, pointed to Daddy in agreement. He swallowed what he could of his mouthful of food and pushed the rest into the left jaw. "I was right here in New York doing construction work, but I couldn't get into the union, even though I wanted to because union pay scale is higher than the regular laborer's." He swallowed the rest of his food and washed it down with iced lemonade. "Every day I asked the white foreman about getting in, and every day he'd say they weren't taking any new people then. After a while I see this white foreign guy—just moves to America and couldn't speak English—showing off his new union card to the foreman. The foreman was all smiles and talking another language with this guy. Right then I knew what time it was—and that's why I'm a mortician today.

"That foreman and the union were 'civilized,' " he said, mocking Aunt Emma's use of the word. "They didn't say, 'We don't take Negroes in the union!' They just didn't. Now, you tell me the difference."

Aunt Emma had no answer. So much for civilization.

Mommy changed the subject, and Aunt Emma gladly obliged.

"You mail my chain letter yet?" she asked.

"You mean you sent me that letter?" Aunt Emma exclaimed. "The plumbing in my house needs fixing, my car's broke, my puppy can't get house-trained, and you're sending me chain letters threatening me with more bad luck? Please!

"I got one of those letters from a numbers man once. It said, 'Look in your wallet and take out the biggest bill and mail this letter on. . . . Don't hold up the blessing.' "

"Did you mail it?" I asked.

"Sure, I did. Didn't put any money in it, but I mailed it. Wouldn't want to hold up somebody else's blessing!"

Aunt Emma made Mommy laugh like normal, and I was glad.

All the time we were doing the dishes, I was looking at Aunt Emma, wanting so bad to talk to her. The couple of times she caught me staring, I just smiled. She smiled back, probably wondering if her niece was flipping, but she didn't say anything. I had put the food away before starting the dishes, so when we finished, I was ready to go. Aunt Emma would be gone by the time I came back, and still I had not asked her to help with . . . I didn't know what. Only she and I were left in the kitchen; she was humming and running the cold water for a drink; I was just standing there.

"Aun—" "Sher—" we said at the same time.

"You go first."

"No, no, honey, say what's been on your mind so all afternoon."

"I need to talk to you, but I can't right now."

"Oh, I see." She nodded, but she didn't see. I didn't, and if I didn't, who would? The twins? Darin might. "Why don't you come by the office after school tomorrow. I have a wake on Tuesday afternoon."

"Okay. I'll see you tomorrow. Thanks." I kissed my aunt. She smoothed my hair down.

"See you later, sweetheart."

Mommy came in on the tail end of that, wondering, I know, what that was all about.

"I finished the kitchen. May I go out now?"

She looked around the clean kitchen, really wanting to ask what we had been talking about, but saying slowly, "Looks fine. Okay, you can go, but don't let the sun beat you home."

The twins weren't home yet. I walked up Albany Avenue toward Darin's house. He only went to church on holidays. With Easter just past, he wasn't due again till Christmas. He was probably home. *Mommy would die if she knew I was going to a boy's house. No, she wouldn't.* You *would die.* I hoped he was outside playing because I really didn't know where he lived. I knew the block, and that was it. Although the sun was out, a chill hung in the air and a constant breeze stirred it. I zipped up my ski jacket as far as I could without putting on the hood and dug my hands into the pockets.

A block away from Darin's and not a kid in sight. Dag, where was everybody? Except for the painted borders on windows and doors, the three-story brick houses lining the street were identical. I slowed down and wished he'd come bopping out of one of these doors. He didn't. *The projects. Oh, yeah.* There's a baseball field on the Schenectady Avenue side of them. I walked up the street and into the Albany Avenue Housing Projects, a square block of high-rise apartments whose landlord was the City of New York. Here were the kids. Little girls jumped rope and played hopscotch on the cement sidewalks surrounding a huge lawn, where older kids ran. I couldn't see the field, but all of these little kids outside playing boosted my hopes for finding Darin in the ballpark.

"Hi, Sheryl!" A little girl with a head full of ribbons tore away from a game of jump rope to tackle me.

"Hi!" My Sunday school teacher's daughter scuttled under my arm, grabbing it and wrapping it around her like she was a Maypole. I held her hand. Funny, we were just together a few hours ago, but now we smiled as though we hadn't seen each other in years.

"Where do you live?"

"Right there! Mommy!" she screamed up to a third-floor window. "Mommy!" Her mother appeared at the closed window. I waved. Smiling and closing up her sweater, she opened the window.

"Hi, Sheryl! Who are you visiting around here?"

Oh, oh. She'd be on the phone to Mommy in a minute if she knew I was around here looking for some boy.

"A friend from school."

"Where does she live?"

Oh, Lord. She was smiling and hugging her arms against the cold. I was smiling in the cold and getting ready to sweat. *Say something, girl.*

"Excuse me?" I put my hand up to my ear as though I didn't hear her the first time. *Jesus, please.*

She waved her hand to say "never mind." "Better go on—it's going to be dark soon." She waved; I waved. *God, I thank you.*

"You know her?"

"Huh?"

"You know Tina?" one of her friends asked me, her mouth hanging all open. *Boy.*

"Yeah."

"You her cousin or something?" *Oh, I get it.* She was only nine, but the oldest of three.

"Yeah, she's my godsister. My favorite godsister."

"Yeah, she's my godsister. My *big* godsister."

"Oh," they said, probably rethinking thoughts of ever bothering her.

"See ya, Tina!" I kissed her on the forehead. "Bye, y'all."

"Bye."

Outside I sort of laughed, but inside I sure hoped none of them had any bigger sisters, or cousins.

A group of boys leaned against the wire fence that surrounded the ball field on Schenectady Avenue. I couldn't tell if a game had just started or ended, but they weren't playing now. I strained to make out Darin, but he wasn't there. Now who would help me figure out what I needed Aunt Emma to help me with? *Girl, shut up and go closer—you'd need binoculars to see him from here!*

Closer and closer. No Darin, but plenty of "Hey, girl, you looking for me?"

"Naw, man, she looking for me, right, baby?"

"You cute—come here."

Don't go a step closer. Don't act scared.

"Y'all know a boy named Darin Fogey?"

"Darin! Whoa."

"Yo, Darin! There's a girl over here looking for you, man! Hey, girl, what's your name?"

"Sheryl!"

"She said her name's Sheryl!"

Closer to the fence I could see three boys in a triangle throwing a baseball. There was Darin, a familiar face really glad to see me. He threw the ball to one of the other guys and did a slow run/walk off the field while his friends hooted.

"Whoa, Darin!"

"Can I get it!" They did so much slapping five, it sounded like fast song clapping at church. I tried so hard not to smile, my cheeks hurt. Darin climbed through a hole cut out of the wire fence.

"Hi, Darin."

"Hi, Sheryl." He touched my elbow just a little, and we started toward the swings, him walking with a hip bop so deep I wanted to ask him if his foot hurt. I didn't, though—that would have spoiled everything.

"Don't mind my friends. They're crazy." He stuck his hands in his pockets and talked to me while looking at everything else—the sky, the buildings, traffic, his shoes. "So what're you doing around here?"

"Looking for you."

He looked up at me. "Yeah?"

"The twins aren't home, and I needed to talk to somebody bad." Well, the twins weren't home. Besides, this boy didn't need to be getting a big head, thinking I came around here because I liked him or something. *And you don't?*

"Oh." He didn't buy it either; he sounded *too* sincere. Forget it.

Darin sat on the swing like it was a horse, crosswise and facing me. It swayed from side to side, coming close to mine, but not touching. I brushed my bangs down with my hand. They rolled back up.

"Spring bangs."

"Boy—"

"No, your bangs are like a spring. You pull them down, they spring back up." He pulled them down, and sure enough, they did. "Ping! That's cute."

Our hands clashed at my bangs, me trying to brush them down again, him trying to make them go "ping" again. *Tonight, I won't roll them; maybe they'll lie down.* I know cute when I see, and spring bangs aren't cute; he's just being nice.

"You got a boyfriend around your way?"

"Huh?" *You can't hear him? If he gets any closer, he's going to be sitting in your lap.*

"Or in your church?"

"No."

"How come?" *Dog if I know.* I shrugged. "I know a lot of guys must try to talk to you." *If you don't say something quick, this boy's going to ask you to go with him. So, you like him, right? I don't know. I mean, he's all right, but—*

"Sheryl—"

"Darin, I need your help with something." *Whew!*

"Oh, okay." He stopped his swing with his feet.

"I know where we can raise a lot of money for the freedom riders."

"Yeah, how?"

"Not how, I don't know how. But I know where: in church. I was hoping you would be able to help me figure out how."

"Me? You're the one who goes to church every day of the week."

"I don't go to church every day of the week. Listen, today they raised five hundred fifty dollars."

"Whew!"

"And half of that was for a guest speaker they didn't even know!"

"So what's your problem? Just have them take up an offering." I sucked my teeth. "What's wrong with that?"

"Nothing, I guess. But what do *we* do then?"

"Count the money."

"The trustees do that."

"Collect it, then."

"The trustees do that too."

"Tell people to give the money."

"My Aunt Emma does that best. She's the one who raised all that money today. She sang for the Mothers, then slipped into the offering. Weaved her song all round it. Before anybody knew it, they gave two hundred dollars to the guest speaker."

"Who?"

"I forgot his name. Some minister from out of town."

"Well, the main thing is to get the money, right?"

"Yeah."

"It's more than we'd get selling candy, right?"

"Yeah."

"Settled."

But it wasn't. A waiting followed me to bed and woke me in the morning. It hovered quietly while I told the twins about the special offering on the way to school, then spoke through Pam.

"And . . .?"

"And what?" I said, even though I knew.

"And what else? You're going to take an offering and that's it?"

I shrugged.

"You can ask your aunt Emma to sing and raise the offering," Pat said. We waited.

"What if we have a spring concert like they do at school every year, except Aunt Emma would raise an offering," Pam said.

"Who'd sing? Me, you, and Sheryl? Who'd pay to hear that?"

"A spring concert," I said. "A freedom concert. Pam, maybe you could play."

"No, she can't!" Pat screamed. "Not if you want somebody to be giving their money for it. Somebody might pay her *not* to play!"

"If she practiced . . ."

"No, Sheryl. Pat's right on this one."

We went to class, waiting. When nothing else came by

lunchtime, the spring concert idea started looking better. We ruled out a trio—we were not the Supremes—but we all sang in choir. Still, who would pay to hear that, especially with Pam playing? To tell the truth, she was pretty good once she got going, but she hardly ever got going. She starts and stops and starts and stops as she makes mistakes; and she can't just pick up in the middle; she has to go back to the beginning. Our whole block knew that much from hearing her practice. How do you put a concert together anyway? And who all would sing in this choir? What would we sing? Where would we practice? Where would we have a concert? When? So many things. Maybe we should just raise an offering to buy candy and sell that.

"Now, that's stupid! Raising money to buy candy to raise less money than you could just raising it!" George hollered when we brought it up at lunchtime.

"No, Sheryl. The concert could work. We just have to get a good musician to pull the music together. Somebody who knows how to make a choir work," Pam said.

"You could do that, Pam."

"No!" Pat jumped all over the tail end of Darin's suggestion. "We need somebody who's *good*."

"Then we sure don't want the organist from my church," I said. "Everything she plays sounds like a march. Bom-bum, bom-bum, bom-bum, bom—"

"There's a guy who plays in my church. He is"—Pam searched for words—"so smooth. He is so sweet. He is so—"

"Dag, Pam, you talk like the boy is cheesecake," I said.

"Better! His playing, I mean. When he plays, I'm telling you, the church starts jumping. Our pastor makes him stop when people start shouting, to keep them from dancing to his music. I mean this guy is so—"

"All right, we believe you," I said. "Could you get him to play for us?"

Pam looked doubtful, but Pat said, "We'll get him."

By the end of the school day, we all had assignments. George and Darin were recruiting kids for the choir, the twins were getting the musician—we hoped—and I had to get a place to rehearse and hold the concert, and Aunt Emma.

Our plan to help the freedom riders was going to work! I ran to the funeral home at three o'clock.

11 🔲🔲🔲🔲🔲🔲🔲🔲🔲🔲🔲🔲🔲🔲🔲🔲

"How's somebody gonna name their child Jezebel?'' I asked, peering over Aunt Emma's shoulder at "Home-going'' service programs for Jezebel Coriander Pitts, who, according to the ancient photo, had been a pretty young woman who was now old and dead. Aunt Emma placed the folded programs in a box labeled PITTS and put them in the Tuesday file behind her desk.

"I don't know, but her mama laid it on her, and she lived right on up to it till the very end!''

"What'd she do?''

"What didn't she do?'' Aunt Emma laughed. "Please now, don't ask me anything else about that woman, because I might tell you. Then your father will kill me, and I'll be laying up in a room like this, and some child'll come in there asking why my mama named me Emma!''

Aunt Emma took off her black suit jacket and jocose manner. She pulled a chair nearer to her desk. "Come—

sit down." She smiled lightly, smelling of rosewater. "What's on your mind?"

I explained. Aunt Emma listened intently, not only with her ears, but with soft, brown, always-moist eyes that believed me more than I did.

"They need the money—and not just for bail and medical care. A lot of them are students like Uncle Pete and working full-time in the civil rights movement instead of getting paid this summer. They won't be able to afford school come September. There's a whole lot of things they'll need."

"Of course. Do you-all have a dollar goal set?"

"No, but they raised two hundred dollars for that guest speaker on Sunday!"

Aunt Emma laughed a little but quickly sobered. "You need to set a goal so you have some kind of idea of what you're reaching for. You'll never reach it if you don't know what it is. I'd say no less than two thousand dollars," she said without blinking.

"Two thousand dollars!"

She shrugged. "There's a lot of money out there, Sheryl. You just got to know where to go to get it. Everybody's seen what's happening to those kids. They'll be more than happy to do anything they can to help, so long as it's not too much."

"Giving money beats going to jail or getting bit by dogs."

"There you go." She pointed at me the same way Daddy does when you give him the answer he wants to a question with more than one answer.

"Okay, Sheryl, so what do you want me to do?"

"Help us."

"Of course I'll *help you*. But I'm not going to *do it*. Your words say *help*, but your tone says *do this*."

"No, no, I'm going to help."

"No, no, *I'm* going to help. You and your friends are going to have to do it or it won't get done, let's understand that now."

"Understood." I smiled.

"Good. So what do you want me to help with?"

"Everything."

"You didn't understand what I said."

"No, I understood, Aunt Emma, but we never did this before. So we'll need your help with all of it."

"Where are you going to have the concert?"

"Oh, that's one of the things I was supposed to ask you about. Could you get Pastor and the trustees to approve it for us so we can do it at the church?" Aunt Emma was the church's first and only woman trustee. "We need to do it before the end of June, when people start taking vacation."

"The church calendar is full, Sheryl, but I'll bring it to the trustees' meeting this week. We'll see."

She reached her hand out over her desk to shake mine. "Okay, Sheryl, I'm recruited. Watch out, Jim Crow, the Williams women are on the case!"

I walked up Fulton Street away from the funeral home, tingling all over. It was working! When I turned down Kingston Avenue, I ran, not because I was late, and boy was I, but because I'm too big to be skipping in the street. I was running so fast, I almost missed the twins, draped over monkey bars in the park. They had already gone home and changed.

"Sheryl!" Pam called. Pat was engrossed in the basketball game in the court across from us. "What happened to you after school? You ran out the classroom. Didn't even say bye.''

"Sorry. Guess what—"

"That's him, Sheryl. The tall one." Pam whispered as though the boy might really hear her words over all the noise of the avenue and park.

"That's who?" I whispered to keep her company.

"Alton Johnson, our organist. Where'd you say you went after school?"

"To see my aunt Emma."

"How'd it go?"

"She's on! She really liked the idea and everything."

"Good! Now, if we can just get Alton." Pamela breathed deeply and turned to Pat.

On Sundays Alton Johnson played the organ at the twins' church, but on weekday afternoons he played basketball in the park at Kingston and Atlantic avenues. His face glistened with sweat as he ran up the concrete basketball court with a lay-up. Swoosh! The rim of the net shuddered as the ball dropped in for two points. Pamela and Patrice waited for the twenty-one-point one-on-one game to end.

"How are we going to do this?" Pam's so scared of everything.

"Ooh, did you see that? Sixteen. That boy, his playing is ferocious!" Pat said.

"Maybe we should wait and ask him while we're at church," Pam said.

"Eighteen. We need to know before Sunday if he's going to play for us because we have to start rehearsing Saturday. Your aunt's getting the church for us, right, Sheryl?"

"She said she'd try."

"So, how are we going to do this, Patrice?"

"What do you mean, 'How are we going to do this?' We'll just go up to him after the game and ask him. Boy, you act like he doesn't know us."

"He knows us in church. We're in the park now."

Patrice sucked her teeth at Pam. "You haven't changed much since Sunday, Pam."

"You know what I mean."

"Pam, please. After he loses this game, we're going to go over to him and ask him if he'll play for the benefit concert. What is so hard about that? Stop worrying." Just then, the short guy sank a three pointer from outside the key. "Come on. He just lost to a short guy. He'll be glad for us to rescue him off the court. Alton!"

"Don't yell, Patrice. Let's just walk over there."

Pat ran on; Pam, reluctantly, and I followed. With all the screaming Alton still apparently had not heard. And the twins, with a question on their minds, didn't even notice the argument Alton was having with a smart-mouthed boy on the sidelines. When we got about five feet from him, he heard Pat screaming his name and turned around and angrily yelled, "What!" We stopped short, bumping into one another. Nothing came out of Pat's open mouth, so Pam softly filled in.

"Hi. Please, let us ask you something."

Alton was pissed. But Pat had been right; he was glad to have somebody besides that smart-mouthed boy on the sideline to talk to after getting beat by a short guy. He stared at Pam—although to me his eyes said he wasn't really listening—while she explained what we were trying to do. He took her number on a tiny piece of paper, sure to get lost, and said he'd get back to her on it. It didn't look good.

On the way home, Pam promised to practice—she might have to be the musician after all. Pat groaned. I checked my watch: four-thirty. Darin was in the middle of practice.

"Would y'all walk me to the ball field over by Albany Projects before we go home? I have to tell Darin something."

The twins looked at each other.

"Oh, don't start."

"We didn't say a thing."

"Just because you sat next to Darin Fogey all day today, and will again tomorrow, and 'haa-ave to' tell him something else *right now*, it doesn't mean anything, does it, Pat?"

" 'Course not."

"But tomorrow, while you're sitting next to him all day, why don't you get his phone number so that the next time you just 'haa-ave to' tell him something we all won't have to walk over to the ball field with you!"

"Well, next Sunday, why don't you get Alton Johnson's telephone number!"

"To do what?" Pat screamed. We all laughed. The only way the twins could call anybody was out the window. Their mother said telephones were for grown people who paid the bill—period.

We were still laughing when we saw Darin playing second base, chewing raspberry Now-or-Laters, waiting for the next hit. He always chooses raspberry flavor now. And sometimes he's even sweet as a raspberry. He saw us and waved. I was positive he was having no problem with *his* job; people enjoy going along with his ideas. He's got it like that. We climbed through the hole in the wire fence and watched him work.

"Can you sing?" he asked the guy who'd landed on second, not taking his eye off the pitcher's mound.

"Huh?"

"Can you sing? What's the matter, you deaf?"

"I ain't no Temptation, but I can carry a tune. Why?"

"That's all it'll take. We're having a concert to raise money for the freedom workers. Come by that church on St. John's Place. I'll let you know when."

"Oh, I could probably do that. My—" The next guy up to bat bunted, creating single base moves. One out was made in the process, but someone had again landed on second. Darin popped another raspberry Now-or-Later in his mouth.

"Can you sing?"

I bopped into the house three hours late and singing the 4-Tops' "I Can't Help Myself." Mommy looked at me, then the clock, and said, "You better."

"You know what we need? Fliers." Darin's neat handwriting leaned across the top margin of my notes on the War of 1812. Aunt Emma had called with good news before I left for school. The trustees approved the concert and cleared Saturday, June 15, anytime after 3:00 P.M., for it. We had a lot of work to do in a little bit of time.

Aunt Emma said that if we were going to get the two thousand dollars we were shooting for, we couldn't rely on by-chance offerings. We needed to get people to make pledges that would be due by concert night. We needed donations from other churches, organizations, and neighborhood stores.

But first we had to get the word out.

I was writing "I can make one tonight, but—" when the lunch period bell rang. I finished my note aloud. "What should be on it?"

"You're the artist."

"No, I mean words."

"Words for what?" Pam snapped her rubber book band and leaned against our desk.

"Sheryl's going to make a flier tonight about the concert."

"What should it say? I mean besides the date and place and all."

"Freedom Rider Benefit Concert."

" 'Free-will donations will be taken. Make your pledge today. Call St. John's Place Church,' and give the telephone number," Darin added.

"If I make it tonight, we can probably mimeograph it tomorrow at the funeral home—"

"Huh, *you* can mimeograph it at the funeral home." Pam and Darin laughed and slapped five.

"You don't have to be afraid of dead people."

"I won't, because I'm not going to be there," Pam said, still laughing.

"Boy." I smirked, but to tell the truth, I don't like funeral homes either, not even Aunt Emma's. I'm not afraid—it's just something about the smell of all of those live flowers around dead bodies that always makes me want to leave. "Anyway, if we have them in time for our first rehearsal this Friday, the choir can start handing them out over the weekend."

"I'm just kidding," Darin said. "I'll help you—even in a funeral home." He made a lemon-taste face.

"Well, I'm serious. I'm not going to be there. Now, if your church has a machine, I'll help, but otherwise . . ." Pam did a thumbs-down.

"That's okay, Pam. We don't want to upset our musician."

Pam's face twisted. "Don't remind me."

Music was a problem from the start, since we had to squeeze rehearsals in around the church's regular choirs.

Too much was happening at the church for us to have a Saturday rehearsal, so our first practice came at 6:00 P.M. Friday. And even that almost had to be at the twins' house because the ushers met on Friday night and didn't want the disturbance—but Aunt Emma *helped*.

After school Craig went with me to the funeral home to pick up the three hundred fliers Darin and I had stayed copying till nine o'clock the night before. Uncle Walter drove us home after, but Mommy said she still didn't like that hour on a school night. She tried to sound half-mad, I guess because she thought she ought to, but I could see she wasn't really—we have the same talking eyes. And when I asked her about helping to get donations from some stores, she had hardly answered yes before she was ticking off the businesses near her and Daddy's beauty/barber shop.

Now I sat in the choir loft, waiting and feeling everything: scared that nobody would come, excited that everybody would come, and unsure that I'd know what to do with them when, and if, they did come. I was nervous that we'd have only Pam for our musician. In short, I was exhausted.

Kids from the junior choir trickled in first. Then the twins. Pam went straight to the piano. She was playing with minor chords when Alton Johnson walked in. I looked at Pat. Her face brightened. Now, even if the choir sounded a mess, Alton's organ would make the concert worth the people's while. Pamela rose from the piano when she heard warm gospel organ chords backing up her light tinklings. She nodded hello to Alton and started for the choir loft, but he beckoned her to stay. Confused, she pulled the hood down over the piano keys, thinking that's what Alton was trying to tell her. She turned to leave again.

"No, Pamela, sit down and play."

"He knows my name," Pam whispered to me.

"Good. Now he can call *you* out the window!" I whispered, my back to the organ.

"But we're getting ready to start."

"I know." Alton laughed a little. "You can do it."

"No, I can't. I make too many mistakes."

"So did I at first. Sit down. You're the other musician for this group." Nervous and happy, Pam sat down and continued playing. Pat moaned. I shrugged. Maybe Alton's playing could cover the mistakes to come.

By six, the spacious choir loft was filled. Most of the junior choir members were there, but there were more: Craig and his high school friends, George with kids from his block.

And just as we were going to start, Darin and his softball team came in—straight from practice, though they really should have gone home first—giving the happy laugh that had been welling up in me for nearly half an hour a good excuse for coming out. Darin plopped down beside me on the pew.

"Hi, Sheryl."

"Hey, Raspberry."

12 ◻◻◻◻◻◻◻◻◻◻◻◻◻◻◻◻◻

I think I might be Darin's girlfriend now. Nothing definite, but it's possible. The last three weeks have made anything possible to me.

There are one hundred kids in choir. One hundred. We overflow the loft and fill the Mother Board's pews. Right now, I am measuring lines for a chart of financial pledges made and paid, to post in the church lobby. We have five hundred dollars—so far. Smooth, mellow piano chords drift from the sanctuary upstairs into my Sunday school room turned concert office, where we are working. Pam is practicing, alone.

Darin is using two fingers to type concert invitation letters to civil rights groups. He stares intently at the paper as he slowly pecks letters onto it. He is chewing the inside of his mouth—he must have run out of Now-or-Laters. When he catches me looking, I don't look away—I just smile. He smiles too, and we go back to our work.

Anything is possible.

The weeks are whirlwinds, and so much is happening. Even in me. Something's changing, and not like the gradual shift of seasons, but fast and heavy so you can't help but notice. I feel it so strong, I keep waiting to see something in the mirror. I don't know. It's not that I've turned fly. I postponed those plans till after the concert. I just don't have the time. Between school, home, and concert work, I hardly have time to go to the bathroom good, let alone get fly. After the concert. Wonder if Darin will still like me fly.

"Should I type this on a stencil or regular paper?" Pat stood in the middle of the room holding up a handwritten concert announcement to send to the newspapers and radio stations.

George said, "Stencil. Especially if you type as slow as Darin."

"I type better than you," Darin said. "And I'll be typing better than everybody before this concert is over."

"Shoot, you won't even be finished typing that letter before this concert is over—"

Darin threw one of the many crumbled papers surrounding his end of the table at George. He ducked. It hit Pat in the face.

"War!" somebody shouted, and it was on. I rushed to Darin's papers and threw two at Pat. The second one hit her. George was returning the shots across the table.

Parker picked up a Magic Marker microphone. "Fighting erupted today on the home front. And, ladies and gentlemen, it's a grisly, grisly sight."

"We're running out of ammunition!" Darin called. George and I dashed under the table and fought over paper balls.

107

"Get away! Get away!" I pushed George away from the papers cradled in my arms and threw them back toward Darin's feet. "Darin! Take these!"

George lunged after them but banged his head on the tabletop first. I laid right on out under the table, laughing. A piece of paper flew by the door just as someone walked in.

"Sister Monroe! I'm sorry. Are you all right?"

I would have stayed hidden under the table if George's yelping hadn't already got her to peer down there.

"Sheryl," she said, as though she wasn't bending down and talking to me under a table, "y'all come on to the office."

"Aunt Emma." *You're on all fours. Wait till you're standing, for crying out loud.* "Aunt Emma, really we were working hard up to about five minutes ago, right?"

They nodded.

Aunt Emma, her half-moon eyes smiling, stood sideways in the door while we filed out past her. "I know."

"So why do we have to go to the office?" I asked.

"Pastor wants to see y'all about something else."

"We didn't do it."

"You didn't do what, Darin?"

"Whatever you're taking us to the office for!"

The office was empty, but the door to the pastor's study was open. He was on the phone, nodding, forehead all wrinkled.

Pam came in. "Brother Sexton told me come down. What happened?"

I shrugged.

Aunt Emma stepped into the pastor's study. "Okay, they're all here now."

Pastor covered the receiver with his hand. "Sheryl, you come in here. Twins, you too. You boys pick up in the office."

The twins and I scrunched up next to one receiver. "Hello."

A deep, sweet, southern voice broke through light static. "Hey, Sheryl. How's my favorite niece in New York?"

"Uncle Pete! It's my uncle Pete, twins."

"Whoa!" Uncle Pete interrupted the chorus of "Hi, Uncle Pete"'s that followed. "Just Pete, please. Y'all make it sound like I'm Uncle Remus!"

"Hi, Pete. I'm Sheryl's friend Darin."

"Hi, I'm Pat."

"I'm her sister, Pam."

"They're twins." I stuck that in.

"Parker here."

"How you doing? I'm George."

"All right. I hear y'all are busy these days being freedom workers up North."

"Well, not like y'all."

"But just as important. I'm so proud of y'all I don't know what to do."

I fixed my mouth to tell him I was proud of *him*, and you know what popped out? "I love you, Uncle Pete."

"I love you too, sweetcake."

"Are y'all really getting beat up like we see on television?" Darin asked.

"Hey, brother, they're not using ketchup on the evening news. It's real. And it's worse out here where there are no cameras. That's why what y'all are doing is so important. It makes everyone remember us freedom workers in places that aren't protected by news cameras."

"Pete, do you think you might be able to come up for the concert?" Pat asked.

"That's why your pastor called. We're going to try to work something out."

"Yeah!"

"Good!"

"All right!"

"Well, I better go on now. Don't want to spend my carfare on a telephone call. Plus, we better leave something for when I get to meet you-all face-to-face. I'm really looking forward to that."

"Yeah, us too," Pam said. "We almost know you already from Sheryl talking."

He laughed. "Good things, I hope."

"Great things," said Darin.

"Great?" He laughed. "Sheryl, what you telling these people?"

"The truth."

"My favorite niece in New York! Well, I really better get off this telephone, okay? Bye now."

"Wait, Uncle Pete."

"Yeah?"

I fixed my mouth to say "Be careful," and you know what? Out it came again: "I love you."

"And I love you, Sheryl. Very, very much."

When we hung up, I started to cry. Not a sad cry. Not a happy cry. Just a full one that came so suddenly I didn't have time to go to the bathroom. And I didn't know why.

I couldn't stop—even with everybody looking. The twins were on either side of me, saying, "Don't cry." George stood across the room asking, "What's the matter with her?"

Aunt Emma came to hold me and knead warm circles in my back, saying, "That's okay, that's okay," until it was.

When I pulled away, wiping my eyes, Darin handed me a small paper cup of water. I don't know what makes folk think crying makes you thirsty, but I knew Darin was being thoughtful. I nodded thanks and took the cup with one hand. I held on to Aunt Emma with the other. She talked and played in my hair.

"Pressure has a funny way of sneaking up on you," she said. "You don't even know it's there until it stops you in your track."

There were a lot of things happening—the concert, down South, schoolwork, graduation in a few weeks. Yeah, I guess it really was a lot.

"A lot of responsibility comes with trying to pull something off like this concert." Pastor walked over to the window and tilted the venetian blinds enough for us all to see cars passing on St. John's Place. "Do any of you know what a fast is?"

At first we looked at one another but didn't say anything, even though we sort of knew, I think.

I said, "It's when you won't eat—"

"Won't eat?" George exclaimed.

"Until God gives you something that you want," Pat finally said.

"Hmm, no. That's extortion—and it doesn't work on God. A fast is when you don't eat," Pastor said.

"Because you want something else more . . . than even food," Pam finished.

Pastor nodded. "You can start out after something and get so caught up in *what* you have to do that you forget *why* you started. Fasting helps you slow down long enough to remember.''

''I don't know about anybody else, but the only thing not eating makes me remember is how much I want to eat,'' George said.

''That's just why it helps,'' Aunt Emma said. ''You get up in the morning, wash, and get ready for school, but instead of grabbing some toast for breakfast, you say, 'Lord, be with the freedom riders.' ''

''I can't *tell* you to fast, but I can tell you, if you do, when you finish, you'll know that you're not alone in what you have to do,'' Pastor said.

We looked at one another. The twins looked like *maybe*. Darin looked like we were fixing to join Ali Baba and the forty thieves. Parker eyed the door. George licked his lips. Somehow, this felt like foot washing to me.

I was going to do it.

It was Monday, and Tuesday was too close for any of us to say, ''Okay, let's not eat tomorrow.'' We settled on Wednesday till six o'clock—for those who wanted to. If somebody didn't want to, that was cool too. (Parker relaxed.) And on the Wednesday before the concert, we'd ask the whole choir to fast. Pastor said that would help us get on one accord for the concert.

''Ten, nine, eight, seven, six, five, four, three, two—''

We raced to the door of White Castle Hamburgers on Empire Boulevard. Darin made it first, but George screamed, ''I'm first!'' and pulled him back, so Parker scooted in. George had ended up fasting with us after all. The twins and I ran around to the door on the other side.

Aunt Emma had told us to break the fast with something

light, like fruit. But we said later for that—we were hungry—and left for White Castle at five o'clock. We stood outside White Castle smelling those tasty little hamburgers for thirty minutes, waiting for it to turn six o'clock so we could end the fast.

By seven, I was home, in bed, sick as a dog, and slipping into the strangest dream.

First, I'm watching from the earth as a flock of birds gets smaller and smaller in the distance. Then, I am there. I'm not flying with them, but my eyes are there. The birds are speckled black and white and brown and white, and they are squawking to cheer on the one in front. It's tired, though, and wants to switch off being the leader. Finally another bird flies up alongside it and takes over. The old leader squawks thanks and falls back in with the rest. They all shift, like a volleyball game rotation. I drift back to earth and watch their flying formation change.

Then I wake up feeling funny—not happy, not sad, just like I'm waiting for something.

The next morning on the way to school, I asked the twins if they thought the dream meant anything.

Pat said, "Yeah, you shouldn't break a fast with five White Castle hamburgers, fries, and a thick chocolate shake."

13 ◻◻◻◻◻◻◻◻◻◻◻◻◻◻◻

The sky is falling. Uncle Pete is in the hospital.

A dog outside howled just past midnight as though it heard death bells, but really it was the telephone. I knew on the first ring. My stomach dropped like a roller coaster. It rang again and again and again. I hoped so hard it was the wrong number, but I knew better even before Daddy hollered, "Oh, God, no!"

Aunt Minnie Ruth had called with the news. While Uncle Pete was closing up the Hendsonville Freedom School for the night, a bomb exploded, blowing him about fifteen feet away. The shanty school went up in flames. Half a mile away, Hendsonville folk saw and came running. They found Uncle Pete and his co-worker unconscious in an open field.

Craig ran to the bedroom where Daddy cried on the telephone. Slowly, I walked there too. Mommy dropped to her knees. Craig rushed to the bathroom and threw up. I sat cross-legged in the middle of their bed remembering Uncle Pete searching for car bombs at dawn.

I screamed into my parents' pillow.

Morning began in a fog so thick it nearly drizzled. And though it tried, the sun just could not burn through. By noon it was dark as dusk. When the clouds finally jammed, rain fell with the ferocity of Bull Connor's hosings, rain strong enough to do anything—except wash away yesterday. I could see the world laying its burdens down and feeling better, so much better. It began to lighten. *God, did you have a good cry? Me too.* But clouds are recycled puddles. Sooner or later the rains return, just like tears.

After the downpour, the sky stayed gray out of respect. Misty, misty, mourning.

Lord, how about an earthquake? One that swallows up folk who plant bombs in churches and homes and cars and freedom schools. People go looking for them, and all they find be holes. Pickup-truck-sized holes all up and down the highways. Big holes in the ground where they meet to scheme. Little holes in small kitchens where they sit and say grace. . . .

Darin hit me with his elbow. He was trying to hog the desk again. *Today, Darin, you can have it. You can sit in my lap if you want to. Lord—*

"Sheryl!" Darin jammed my math book into my desk and put his social studies text on top in the center as though we were sharing. Mr. Miller was making the rounds. There was a Do Now assignment on the blackboard, but I hadn't even noticed. "Questions number four and five," Darin whispered.

It was from the homework reading. What was Manifest Destiny? How did it affect the growth of the United States? I turned to a clean page, answered the questions, and went back out the window.

Mr. Miller stood over Darin's desk for what seemed like a long time, then read his answer aloud. " 'Something that had to happen.' I see you didn't bother to read the homework, again." He marked a big red *X* on Darin's Do Now, then peered over at my book.

" 'A whitewash'? What's this, a joke? Save your jokes for your friends, She-ryl. I am not amused."

"I'm not joking." The class can hear my heart beat. But I'm not scared—I'm mad. I don't even care. "There's nothing funny about people making like it's God's idea for them to kill and steal from the Indians and make people slaves." I was hot and angry.

Mr. Miller was too. He took a deep breath. "The founders of this country were—"

"Greedy!"

"All they wanted—"

"Was everything! And they made up that Manifest Destiny stuff to—"

I moved my book quickly, and Mr. Miller's red *X* landed on the desk instead of on my Do Now.

"Next time, stick to book definitions, not your opinions."

"It's the truth."

"Not in my book."

Well, this is not your book.

Mr. Miller walked to his desk and pulled out a slip of paper pink as his face. *You know, you don't have any Negro teachers—and never had? That's all Mommy and Daddy had.* The class whispered, while my eye twitched. Darin leaned over and whispered, "It's not so bad." *God, is this happening?*

"You know what else is true, Miss Truth?" Mr. Miller said sarcastically. "You have an appointment with the principal." He motioned to me to come pick up the pink slip. I gathered my books and walked out the back door, leaving the slip in Mr. Miller's hand.

Outside the door, I ran. Down the stairwell right across from Mr. Miller's room and out the building. Up Prospect Place, down Rogers Avenue, across St. John's Place, and why was that bus driver shaking his hands at me? It didn't matter. Outside was cool and felt good against my sweaty palms and neck. No rain, but mist so dense an umbrella, even if I'd had one, wouldn't have helped anyway. No covering my head with books to keep it from napping up. Then, between my chest and throat, came a lump so big, I could see it in my mind. It was red, thick, and glowed. And it grew. And it grew. And when I lifted my face to the sky to show it to God, the clouds burst again.

It was still raining at five after eight the next morning when the doorbell rang.

"Whew, I don't know who was supposed to build the ark this time, but they didn't," Pat said, stamping her feet on the welcome mat.

"You left your umbrella in homeroom," Pamela said, and handed it to me.

"Yeah, I know. Thanks. Y'all are early. Want something to eat?"

"No, thanks, we already ate," Pat said. They looked at each other, then whispered, "Are you going to school today?"

"Yeah."

"Oh, good, you didn't get suspended!" Pat said.

"Ssh! I didn't go to Mr. Banks. I went home."

"Oh, my God," Pam said.

"What are you going to tell Mr. Miller?" I hunched my shoulders. "Well, maybe he won't ask."

Pam said, "I hope you don't get in too much trouble."

"Thanks."

Pat shook us out of the moment's worry. "Okay, Sheryl, you're our best other friend, but not so best a friend that we're gonna be late for you after we left our house extra early, and in the rain, to bring you your umbrella. Get your stuff and let's go, already."

We walked silently through the light rains. And although I could think of nothing else, somehow I did not have the energy to tell my best friends why Manifest Destiny was a sham. Nor that Uncle Pete started his day looking for bombs, expecting them.

Over the next week, Uncle Pete's injury rode me like a witch in the night. And not just me, but our whole family. Ronnie's constant whining threatened to drive us all crazy, and Craig and Daddy stopped saying much of anything besides basics like "Morning," "See you later," "Pass the bread, please." Mommy stalked the house with a king-size attitude, and I avoided her like the plague. Joy seeped out of our house through the cracks, like heat in the winter.

Somehow school, rehearsals twice a week, and other seemingly endless work for the concert moved on.

Alton and Pam rearranged some freedom songs that protesters sang on the way to jail to make them swing gospel-style. Pat, George, Darin, and I met at Aunt Emma's house, listening to her massive gospel album collection, searching for other songs. We each took some home to listen to and write out the words of songs chosen.

Saturday was the regular rehearsal day for the church's other choirs, but we learned to make adjustments, like squeezing in before the first or after the last of the church choirs' rehearsals or getting together after school. We put tone-deaf kids like Darin between two strong singers to keep them on key, or at least drown them out. The church made adjustments too. The official board relocated its Tuesday night meetings so that we could practice in the sanctuary, and Wednesday night prayer meeting voluntarily moved to the basement, where members heard and prayed for our wrong notes.

We planned the day's concert tasks over lunch in Lincoln Terrace Park. There were posters to put up, pledge calls to make, and records to decipher. This week, however, it rained, so we worked in the cafeteria.

"George, what is this?" I said, disgusted, trying to read his chicken scrawl. He thought it was funny. " 'Let my knife compensateth me'? What kind of sense does that make?"

"Hey, I didn't write the song—I just wrote what I heard on the record."

"No, you didn't either. The words are 'Let my life consecrated be.' "

"Well, if you already knew the words, why'd you have me listen to that stupid record over and over and over, trying to figure them out!" George stormed away from the table. Pat called after him, but he walked on. Good riddance.

Then the strangest thing happened. Pat turned on me. "What's the matter with you?" she said angrily, glaring at me.

"We only have two weeks left for—"

"Everybody knows how many weeks we have before the concert. You still don't have the right to go off on somebody like that! You've been turning into a little Napoleon here lately, like you're the only one who knows anything or cares about anything, and we're tired of it! So you'd best check your attitude!"

"*My* attitude? He had an assignment just like everybody else, he didn't do it right, then had the nerve to laugh about it. And I need to check *my* attitude?"

"You know it's hard to understand what choirs are singing half the time. At least he brought something in for us to work with. We can make up words that make sense if we have to—just like we've been doing!"

"Oh, yeah? Well, I don't think any old thing is good enough." I picked up my books and left the table. This wasn't just a project. People down South were putting their lives on the line every day, Uncle Pete was near dead, and George couldn't even pay enough attention to get the words to a simple song straight. Later for these people. I marched out of the cafeteria and away from my friends for what ended up being a week that seemed like a lifetime.

I'd barely made it to the stairway when a voice interrupted my thoughts.

"Do you have a hall pass?" Mr. Miller and Mr. Banks stood outside stairwell number 3, waiting to catch kids trying to cut fifth period. I made a U-turn and was headed back to the cafeteria when Mr. Miller remembered the referral return slip I never gave him.

"Speaking of passes," he said, "She-*ryl*, come here for a minute. Where's the referral return from your meeting with Mr. Banks on Tuesday?" *Oh, brother*.

"A pass from me?" Mr. Banks asked, acting as though this was the most shocking news of his life. "This young lady has not been to my office this week."

"Of course she has. I sent her on Tuesday. You went, didn't you, She-ryl?"

"No, sir." *I don't know why you're whispering now. You're in trouble already.*

"Speak up!" he demanded. "Did you say no?"

"Yes."

"Are you calling Mr. Banks a liar?" *Oh, they're having big fun this afternoon.*

"No."

"Yes or no, which is it!"

"Yes, I said *no* when you asked me if I had gone to Mr. Banks's office the other day."

This was getting stupid. Still feigning amazement, Mr. Banks said he'd never seen me in his office.

"I said I didn't go."

Fifth-period bell rang, and I headed for the stairs. They pulled out the stops. "Where do you think you're going? Get back here, young lady," Mr. Banks yelled. "In my office—now!" The hall was filled with students going to their next class. I set my eyes straight ahead and walked into the office, trying to ignore his ranting, their stares, the fear growing in my belly.

In eight years of school, not counting kindergarten, I'd never been behind the low gray-green steel gate that separated school office workers from the student waiting area. Mrs. Cornell, the stern hall and bathroom monitor, examined me over the rim of her half-frame reading glasses. I followed Mr. Banks into his office, sat down, and stared at him.

"What are you looking at?" he asked in that same tone.

"I don't know."

He couldn't decide how he should take that but let it pass. "Does your mother know that you cut classes?"

"I don't cut classes."

"Oh, but you did, young lady. And you have a very nasty attitude."

That word again. I recited my phone number to him, as asked, then joined the sparrow on his window ledge while he dialed. One o'clock, nobody's home. It's okay.

"Hello, Mr. Williams, this is Mr. Banks, the principal at Junior High School Two-Ten." *Good God, Daddy's home!* "I'm calling about your daughter, Sheryl Williams. She's sitting here right now. Do you want to speak to her?" I tried not to look surprised. "I'm afraid your daughter has been cutting class and disturbing her social studies class." *What's Daddy doing home?* "Not only that, but she failed to report to me as directed nearly a week ago." Daddy apparently said he didn't want to speak to me but would take care of the situation when I came home. Mr. Banks, delighted, nodded his head like the spring-neck dog prizes from Coney Island meant for car dashboards. "Yes, Mr. Williams, it is very important for parents to nip this type of behavior in the bud. Good talking with you."

He hung up the telephone with a smirk for me that said, "You're going to get it tonight, smart ass."

"Get a late pass from Mrs. Cornell and go to your next class. I'd watch my step if I were you."

I opened his office door and went to Mrs. Cornell's desk for the pass.

"She-ryl Williams." She wrote out the pass and slowly

said my name wrong, trying to recall it. "What homeroom is that?"

"Mrs. Weinberg."

"That's a good class." She handed me the note. Then, in a voice that was awfully nice for Mrs. Cornell's sour mouth, she said, "Honey, don't make trouble for yourself."

I took the pass and walked out, wondering what in the world Daddy was doing home in the middle of the day.

When I got home, Daddy was chopping onions and bell peppers on a narrow wood board as Mommy rinsed sliced potatoes and carrots in the sink.

"Hi, Mommy. Hi, Daddy."

"Hello, Sheryl."

"Hey, baby."

Baby? Daddy went back to chopping without a mention of the phone call. What's this? I *know* Daddy hadn't forgotten a call about me from the principal. Were they planning a surprise attack? No, Daddy doesn't play that. If he's going to get you, you're just got. Maybe Mr. Banks had dialed the wrong number after all. I didn't know what was going on, but I wasn't staying around to find out.

As soon as I had thrown my books on the floor and myself on the bed, Craig came into my room and closed the door behind him.

"Cutting classes, Sheryl? I'm so disappointed." Craig laughed in whispers. "Who do you think you are, me?"

"Mr. Williams?"

"In person."

"That's right, you are Mr. Williams."

"Yes, I'm Mr. Williams. I'm a strong disciplinarian and

I assure you this will never happen again," Craig spoke officially into an invisible telephone.

"Well, that's one good thing that happened to me today. The only one."

"What happened?"

"Mr. Miller sent me to the principal's office on Tuesday."

"Tuesday? Today's Friday."

"I know. I didn't go."

"Whoa!"

"I came home instead. It's a long story, Craig, a long stupid story. I'll tell you later. I don't feel good right now." I pulled the pillow under my head. Mommy called from the kitchen.

"Oh, leave me alone! She acts like she only has one child!"

"Hey, don't start that mess—you owe me, Sister."

"Sheryl!"

"Whatever happened, don't make a habit out of it. Your father or, worse, your mother might answer the phone next time."

"Sheryl!"

"You better get hopping." He closed the door behind him. Boy, I wanted to stay, but I dragged myself to the kitchen.

"Where were you?" Of course, she didn't give me a chance to answer or to tell her I didn't feel well. "Mix the salad. And listen, next time I call you, answer—right then, not the next day. I'm too tired for this."

The telephone saved me from her nagging on. I picked it up on the first ring.

"Hello."

"Hey, Sheryl."

"Debra Jean!"

"Debra Jean? What happened? Give me the phone." Mommy started toward the phone, but I put my shoulder between us.

"She called for me." I didn't know if that was true or not, but it kept me from getting maimed since what I really wanted to do was slap Mommy across the room for being so daggone rude all of the time these days. I walked into the hallway, as far away from the kitchen as the cord would allow.

"They tried to kill my mama today," Debra Jean said in a tight, even voice.

I slumped down the wall to the floor.

"What happened?"

"They tried to run her off the bridge while she was coming home from the lumberyard in Muffesboro."

More, God? More?

"They've had it in for her for a long while. You know my mama don't know how to bite her tongue good. And now that she helped build that Freedom School in Hendsonville and went with Petey down to the courthouse to register to vote, they're going after her."

"Is she all right?"

"She's fine now."

"Is who all right?" Mommy asked. I had been whispering, but I gave up. Aunt Minnie Ruth is her sister, her closest sister. And Mommy looked so sad and worn-out standing by the kitchen door, waiting for a bad word.

"Aunt Minnie Ruth is okay, but they tried to run her off the bridge yesterday."

"Oh, Jesus!" Mommy squeezed her eyes, lips, fists tight to shut out the world, but she couldn't.

"Here, Mommy." She stopped squeezing but barely opened her tired eyes or reached out for the telephone I was handing to her. Daddy took it and pulled her close so both could hear. I went in their bedroom and picked up the other extension.

"She was coming from the lumberyard in Muffesboro when they got after her."

"Who's *they*, Debra?" I asked.

"The crackers, girl—who the hell else?" Daddy answered. I heard him from both the telephone line and the next room. "How'd she get away?"

"A tractor-trailer came on the bridge, and she followed it out."

"Thank God," Mommy said. "Let me speak to her."

"She's asleep."

"How'd . . .? What . . .?" Debra Jean knew what I wanted to ask, and told the story.

"Right after we put up the Freedom School, the sawmill here in Salisboro hiked prices or outright refused to sell wood to Mama. She told them to keep their damn wood— her money was green and she'd take it somewhere else. Going to Muffesboro was inconvenient, but Mama said so was Jim Crow. Everything was fine till yesterday when those pickup trucks followed her.

"She said she felt something was wrong as soon as she pulled out of the yard and two other pickups left with her. One was olive. She hates that color. Reminds her of vomit."

Debra Jean's voice trailed on, and the pictured tale passed before me.

The green truck passed her. Aunt Minnie Ruth teased herself about being afraid and had let her mind drift back to her work in Salisboro when that vomit green pickup, now in front of her, slowed down. She accelerated to pass it, but it switched lanes with her. The driver smiled at Aunt Minnie Ruth through his rearview mirror. He slowed down again, and a rusty red truck behind her sped up, sandwiching her. A third one pulled up alongside her, with the driver honking his horn and moving his mouth. She couldn't tell what he was saying, because of all the noise; still, she knew he cursed her because his eyes raged, darting from her to the road, from the road to her.

Aunt Minnie Ruth almost lost control of the truck, her hands shaking and slick with sweat. When they got to that narrow, rickety, old Tom's Creek Bridge, they took her for a drag!

"Mama said she never saw anything like it before. They forced her near the bridge's metal guardrails. She smelled her tires burning. They tried to push my mama into the river."

Aunt Minnie Ruth screamed, "*Holy Ghost!*"

"An eighteen-wheeler came onto the bridge. Can you imagine that? An eighteen-wheeler on that little bitty bridge?"

It shook the bridge to its foundation like an earthquake and forced the pickup on the right to speed up. Quickly Aunt Minnie Ruth switched lanes behind the tractor-trailer and hugged it all the way home. It went right by her house. They did not follow.

Aunt Minnie parked behind her house to hide, as though they didn't already know where she lived. Drenched in sweat, with her heart beating wildly, she threw loose wood boards around the yard, crying, before succumbing to a breeze that she said put her to sleep.

I knew the kind. One of those warm gentle breezes that

whished around and around shoulders, rocking, whispering, and tickling ears. I knew it.

"When we came home from school, we found her asleep right there in the truck beside her wood. We brought her inside. After she told us what happened, she went back to sleep. She's still sleeping now."

We were all silent with our own images of Debra Jean's story till Daddy breathed. "Good. Let her sleep."

"Debra Jean?"

"Yeah, Sheryl?" All along, her voice was calm. So calm. Too calm to have carried all that it had.

"You all right?"

She thought about it and thought about it. And when she found she couldn't say yes, she grunted "huhn" like the old folks when they can't tell the truth.

"You know you can come up here anytime you want," Daddy said. "You know I'll come get you—I'll come get all of y'all."

"I know, Uncle Robert, and I thank you. But how's a whole family going to run away from home?"

There was nothing left to say but "Call me when Minnie Ruth wakes up. Call me collect," which Mommy added before Debra Jean hung up.

In the kitchen Mommy sat in Daddy's lap, her eyes still closed, telephone dangling by the cord from her limp hand and touching the floor. I took the telephone and returned it to the receiver.

Mommy opened her eyes, but only said, "Sheryl, make the salad."

14 ▣▢▣▢▣▢▣▢▣▢▣▢▣▢▣

A mound of crumpled paper filled the trash can next to the door in my room. The concert program had to be special, but at the rate I was going, it wasn't going to exist at all. I turned on music—it was distracting; turned it off—too quiet. I sat at the desk—too much like school; sat on the floor—too hard. I sat on the bed, talked myself into lying down, and the next thing I knew, I was waking up. It was three o'clock Saturday, and I had nothing to show.

Last Wednesday, when we were supposed to tally pledges and decide how to collect them, I had walked into the office, and they were all laughing, talking, playing lip sync—everything except tallying pledges. If I had asked about the tally and how come nobody was doing it, I would have been "too bossy." The concert was less than two weeks away, we hadn't collected half the money promised yet, and they were playing lip sync, but I'm the one who would have been wrong. I turned around and left. Walking to and from school by myself was lonely, but so was being with the group lately. I decided I'd go to the church only when I had to for rehearsals; all the rest of the concert work I did was from home.

Only nothing was coming. I couldn't get a program cover. Midway through my umpteenth try, Mommy came in.

"I want you to go buy some things at Utica for me."

"Okay, in a minute."

"Don't tell me to wait!" She was fueling her fires. "Look it, miss." I hate it when she starts in with that *miss* mess. "I waited thirty-eight hours for you to decide to be born, and I'm not going to wait another second on you in this life. Now, if you're ready to cross Jordan, tell me to wait again."

Was all of that really necessary? I grabbed my jacket, took her list and money, and gladly got out of the house.

Looking straight ahead to pass the twins' house was an unnatural act. Was that Pat in the window? My heart jumped, and I almost smiled when the venetian blinds rattled. An open window at the twins' house meant they were home. Patrice and Pam were home and I couldn't ask them to come with me to Utica. Running was all that kept me from throwing myself on their steps and crying until everything was the same again.

The store manager locked the glass door behind me, and a tepid breeze began stroking my brow. Utica and Eastern Parkway teemed with honking horns and smoky bus engines. People dressed in spring pastels, having bought the stores out, now strolled and enjoyed the start of an almost summer night. The sun setting over my left shoulder warmed the back of my neck and tinted everything and everybody with a mellow orange glow. I breathed deeply, sighed, and took a step toward home right into Darin Fogey.

Arms folded, he stood in front of me, shaking his head.

"Boy, you surprised me!"

"I don't know why. Walking around with your eyes closed, you shouldn't be surprised if you walk into a bus."

I sighed again and tried to pass around him.

He stepped in my path. "Laugh, Sheryl, laugh! That was a joke!"

I tried, but my lips wouldn't move. A sigh came out instead.

"Dag, Sheryl. Walk me to Carvel." Darin shook his head again and sighed too. "You never were but so much fun, and now you're turning into Hagatha."

Hagatha! That's almost as bad as Jezebel Coriander Pitts! A short laugh as mysterious as a hiccup tripped out.

"What is this? A smile?" Darin touched my chin to turn my face toward his. I turned my head away. Darin popped up on the other side. "And her face didn't break!" I giggled. I hate to giggle. I sighed again. "That's right, fight it, Sheryl. You *can* be miserable."

Just that quick, tears popped up, and I was boo-hoo crying in the street.

"Oh, Sheryl." He dug in his pocket and pulled out a wad of worn toilet tissue, blue from dungaree dye and all stuck together by God knows what. He found a relatively clean spot and turned to dab my eyes. I pulled back.

"Not—my—eyes."

"Nose?" It was running. I nodded. "Better?"

"Uh-huh." I wiped my eyes with the back of my hands.

He put his arm through mine, and we headed for Carvel. "One thing I don't understand is why you can't even joke anymore," he said. "Like you're scared that if you have a good time, it's going to make it worse on Negroes or something."

"How can I laugh with everything happening?"

"I bet your uncle Pete did, before. He did on the phone that day. Remember?"

"Yeah, I remember. 'It ain't ketchup, brother.' " It made me smile again.

"The freedom riders on the news always be singing and clapping and smiling—well, at least till the dogs and police come. They look happy and strong. They look"—he turned toward me—"holy."

"Holy?"

Darin stopped a second and thought. "Yeah, like the Roman gladiator movies, when they're getting ready to—you know what I mean."

"How can they laugh and sing and smile, Raspberry?"

"I don't know. . . . Maybe they believe so strong that when one of them gets down—like you—the others believe for them till they're okay again. But you, you're not speaking to anybody but you, and you're too down to cheer yourself up.

"Look, I know you're worried about your uncle—we all are—and that you're not talking to your best friends. And you're worried about the concert. And all of that is nothing compared to the trouble you're going to have if your folks find out you've been cutting social studies. . . ." He stopped and looked at me, cocking his head like a beagle–German shepherd we used to have. "Never mind, Sheryl. Let me help you in front of this truck." He grabbed my arm and pulled me to the street.

"Boy, let go of my arm."

"It'll be fast, Sheryl. You probably won't even feel it."
He pulled me and waved the truck on. My package fell.

"Wait! My package!"

"Don't worry about it. What's in it?"

"Curtain rods!"

"You won't be needing those where you're going."

"What do you mean? It *is* curtains!" I twisted my arm
loose from his. "Boy, you're sick."

"And you, girl, are laughing!"

Meanwhile, the truck had gotten stuck turning up the
service lane. How that man thought he was going to get his
big old truck up that skinny street was a mystery. Raspberry
and I, laughing so hard we could barely walk, made it to a
parkway bench and watched the driver try to blame it on
the sidewalk, as though it wasn't there before he started that
ridiculous turn. Police came. Traffic stopped. We were almost okay when the police directed the truck driver straight
into a NO PARKING pole. It fell over. By the time we got to
Carvel, which was only across the street, it was night.
Raspberry's soft vanilla ice-cream cone with sprinkles was
too soft. End-of-the-day ice cream dripped over his fingers.
We licked to stop the drip, like second graders. I took the
right side, Raspberry the left. When we met in the middle,
he licked my face, then smiled like Howdy Doody. Ice
cream went down my windpipe. Raspberry left me at Troy
Avenue, and I went, sticky mess that I was, to make up
with the twins.

It was pitch-black outside when I walked into the kitchen
carrying curtain rods and pins wrapped in brown paper.
Craig looked up from the sink filled with soapy water and
dinner dishes.

"Whoa, Sister, where've you been?" he said half-laughing.

"Mommy sent me to Utica." I lifted a pan top. Fish and corn bread.

"Your watch broken?" he asked.

I sucked my teeth. "I don't have a watch."

"Hey, even a sundial could tell you you're a little bit late."

"I don't have a sundial either." I washed my hands and face, then fixed myself a plate.

"And, Sister, I thought even you had sense enough to not go kissing any boys in the middle of Utica Avenue." My corn bread fell back into the pan.

"What? I didn't kiss anybody."

"Then why're you smiling?"

"Because that's ridiculous. If I were going to kiss a boy, I wouldn't do it in the middle of the street, for crying out loud."

"Yeah, well, your mother got another report."

"Huh?"

"You know the neighbors are on duty twenty-four–seven, especially on Saturday. Somebody called Ma and said you were carrying on on Utica like a shameless hussy with some scraggly-looking boy."

"Oh, brother."

"Sister"—he lowered his voice to a whisper—"your ass is grass."

"That was Darin Fogey, and I didn't hardly kiss no Darin Fogey in the middle of the street. We were just talking. Boy, some people need to mind their own business."

"That I know."

"Craig, a big old truck got stuck trying to turn down the

service lane on Eastern Parkway.'' In my head it replayed like a movie, but Craig hadn't seen it, so my story wasn't nearly as funny to him, and I could barely tell it, laughing and snorting like a pig.

"And then the—ha-ha-ha."

"The ha-ha what?"

"The pol—ho-ho."

"The pole came down?"

"That too!" We laughed until Mommy entered the doorway. It's a wonder steam wasn't shooting out her nose and ears.

"Mommy, I don't know who called you, but I didn't kiss anybody in the middle of no—"

"You left out of here four hours ago. Where have you been?" Before I could answer, she asked, "Where are my curtain rods and pins?" I pointed to the corner and started to say "Over there," but she continued. "Let me tell you something, miss, you're not going to run wild in the street. I'm not going to have it."

"Mommy, I—" My ears rang, and red dots floated before my eyes. Her slap made me drop my plate. Fish and corn bread flew over the floor.

"I'm not going to have this! I'm not going to have this!" Mommy screamed over and over, as she hit me a couple more times. She turned like I'd disappeared and started walking up and down the hallway, crying angrily and screaming insanely. Craig and I would have looked at each other, but we were too scared to see what the other was thinking.

"Mommy," Craig yelled. She screamed louder. "Mommy!" She pushed him away. Daddy rushed out of their bedroom in boxer shorts and a T-shirt.

"Ruby! What?" She pushed Daddy away as she had Craig and paced the hallway for a few minutes, which seemed like hours, then finally fell to her knees, exhausted. She leaned against the narrow hall wall and moaned. Over and over, Daddy called her name like you'd pick up fine porcelain, but she paid him no mind. Her moans became softer, and Daddy was fixing to pick her up. Then both her arms flew up, one knocking Daddy in the chin.

"Fa-thah! Fa-thah!" she screamed. "Don't just let him lay. Father, make him well or take him home. *Or take him home.*" She cried like June rains. And after her tears tapered, she rested her head in Daddy's neck. This time there was no protest when he lifted and took her to their room. She held his neck tightly. Craig wept bitterly against the wall. I put my arm around his shoulder and joined him.

The smell of fresh coffee and bacon frying crisp filled the morning in my mother's house. Mommy contentedly hummed a song as she sprinkled cinnamon and raisins over steaming oatmeal and threw bread crumbs out the back door window to the sparrows.

And I wasn't surprised to learn that during the night Uncle Pete had quietly died.

15 ▢▢▢▢▢▢▢▢▢▢▢▢▢▢▢▢

We did not journey back down South in mourning, but in defiance. We packed quickly after breakfast and left with the midmorning sun overhead, daring traffic to hinder. We made no detours to avoid trouble, and gassed up at full-service stations. Around about Richmond, we began singing:

> "Ain't gonna let nobody
> Turn me 'round!"

Going through Hendsonville was the only change we made in our route. Charred grass, scattered wood, and a persistent smell of smoke guided us to where the Freedom School once stood. We walked to what may have been the center of the one-room schoolhouse and contemplated the evil that had destroyed it. Daddy prayed aloud with his eyes open, looking around and gesturing as though God were in our circle of joined hands. He asked for justice. "Mercy has its place, but, God, this ain't it." Mommy laid a small bunch of roses from our backyard on the blackened grass. I closed my eyes and stood real still, trying to feel what it must have been like just a week ago, the shanty school filled with strong wills and spirits and bodies. But all I felt was empty.

Less than thirty minutes later we pulled up to Ma Pudnum's driveway. To our surprise, the house was packed. I had expected the kin and neighbors, who always came with food and hands ready to help the bereaved, to be there sitting with Ma Pudnum, but there were dozens of unexpected others, young people, including the white couple from the Good Friday communion service.

The porch was full of suitcases and people in clergy collars, dungarees, uncomfortable ties, Sunday best. Some had come from nearby towns. Others waited, friendly but tired from long journeys from as far away as Chicago, for home assignments. Strangers, but not really. They were freedom riders.

Word of the bombing had spread rapidly on the freedom "wire," and the students wasted no time in deciding that what Uncle Pete and the folk in Hendsonville started had to continue—and succeed. For if the people who opposed them saw that bombs could stop the work, the murders would have only just begun. And so they enlisted scores of students to pick up where Uncle Pete left off. Every few minutes a car would pull up, load one or two freedom riders, then take off up the road, leaving a red puff of dust behind.

I watched for a while, then wandered slowly through the house, half-seeking a quiet place to rest, half-pretending it was my first time through the winding trail of rooms. There was the black pot-bellied stove, stuck in time and Grandma's room. There was Granddaddy, still chewing on that cigar, looking more like Craig than ever. There was Mommy's old room, her suitcase thrown over the bed with the tall, scary posts she had once shared with Aunt Minnie Ruth. And there was Uncle Pete's room. The door was closed with a note still taped to it: "Call Sister Dickson." A short twist of the knob and a little push opened it.

Uncle Pete's room. I closed the door behind me. It was simple—white panel curtains, mahogany dresser, desk, and headboard. It smelled of damp wood and magnolia blossoms blown in from trees just outside; it smelled of books and papers and man. The made-up bed still had the imprint of Uncle Pete's last late afternoon nap. His farm overalls were folded neatly on top of his dusty boots in the corner near the window. I closed my eyes and inhaled all that was left of Uncle Pete.

Rocks held down two piles of paper on the small desk in front of the window. Under one were a bill for two hundred pounds of fertilizer and newspaper clips of the farmers' market report. Under the other were lists of names and addresses of people from surrounding towns. A sealed overstuffed envelope lay facedown in front of the desk lamp. I propped it back up against the lamp and turned to examine his small bookcase.

Wait!

In neat, evenly slanted print was my name, Sheryl Williams, followed by my address. I sat on the bed and carefully opened the envelope from the back, starting at the unglued ends, slowly working my fingers through the stuck center, trying not to tear it. I stopped to check the name on it again. *Sheryl Williams*. It was mine. *Uncle Pete had written me a letter*. Almost crying, I pulled the thick fold of papers from the envelope. One, two, three, four pages! Four pages? I almost laughed. Uncle Pete might say four whole sentences on a talkative day, and here he is, going out with four pages!

May 19, 1963

Dearest Sheryl,

I've been trying to get a space of time to write to you since Mama told me about the concert you and the other Brooklyn freedom workers are planning to help the effort.

It was good talking with you the other day, but you know I'm not a talker. So I'm writing.

I told you that I was proud of you, and I am. And not just proud, but happy for you. You and your friends have caught sight of the new day whose coming is as sure as the sunrise. I don't have to tell you how rough it's getting down here—you read the paper, you see the TV news. You and your friends renew my hope. I pray and know that God will bless the work of your hands.

As for us down here, things are really coming along. Remember Hendsonville? The place that didn't have a colored school, where that old couple washed our feet. Anyway, about four weeks ago, Minnie Ruth and her clan, the folk in Hendsonville and I fixed up an old barn there to be a school where folk could learn reading and writing and other things. We call it our Freedom School.

Minnie brought some fresh pine planks over in the back of her truck, and the Hendsonville folk had cleared out the barn. We had to dig a hole for all the mildewy mess and mice nests stuck in that place. But after we got all that done, they laid a wood floor, replaced the rusty tin roof, and painted the outside

140

red. Aunt Minnie worked on the floor with some of the men while I led another crew dismantling the roof. People donated tables, chairs, pads, and pencils, and Black Hendsonville started freedom summer.

Debra Jean and some other kids from the high school are teaching the children to read and figure from old primers. It's different with the adults. Many of them have managed to hide their illiteracy through phonographic memories and reading neighbors who help while feigning ignorance. We don't want to shame them by using children's books, so we start with common signs—STOP, SALE, CLOSED, OPEN, POLICE, FIRE, GROCERY. Some of the kids from the high school here are teaching the adults the alphabet and phonics. Using church hymnbooks, they're learning to recognize words to songs sung for lifetimes. Their readers are the Bible and daily newspapers.

Meanwhile, after much "fishing" and preparation, we have a group of people from around the county ready to be registered to vote. Mama, Uncle Enoch, Mama Hemby, Minnie Ruth, and Iris are a part of that group. (Uncle Willie, of course, has refused to go.)

Last week, four carloads of us went to the county clerk's office to register. They've been giving us a truckload of ridiculous reasons for not registering us. Now, a group goes over every day. We'll wear them out yet.

Sheryl, you probably don't know it, but you really keep me encouraged down here in the face of this kind of foolishness. Not just what you and your friends are doing—that too, though. But when I get totally disgusted, you know what I think about? That morning we watched the sunrise together. You asked me why I didn't just leave this place. That's when I realized that I didn't have any place to go to escape this nonsense. No place. Because of the laws down here, the problem is more apparent, but in a way, that's good. I hate shadowboxing.

That song you started singing—the youth fellowship call to worship—reminds me of that morning. I don't know the last time I'd sung that one, but I sing it a lot now.

Well, Sheryl, it's after midnight now, and I worked a full day in the field. I can barely keep my eyes open. So I'm going to sign off.

Love always,
(Uncle) Pete

P.S. I've noticed that you never call me by any name. I'm guessing that's because you can't decide what's appropriate, hence my strange signature. But listen, you can call me anything you feel comfortable with—Peter, Pete, Uncle Pete. Anything except Petey or *nigra*!

Good Lord, Uncle Pete had made a joke!
On the day of the bombing. Maybe just minutes before. I started rereading the letter. And when my heart broke, I held the letter to my chest and went to sleep in Uncle Pete's outline. When I awoke, I sketched the concert flier and program that had been printed in my mind.

Night had fallen by the time I left Uncle Pete's room. I hadn't eaten all day. Aunt Minnie Ruth was serving a too-rich, crumbling cake with coffee to the spattering of people still in Ma Pudnum's kitchen. Four were freedom riders, I could tell. The rest were family, or almost family, like Miss Luella and Mama Hemby. They were planning the movement's next step, between stories of Uncle Pete.

One of the freedom riders was speaking when I came in. "We can't go tomorrow, but by Wednesday—"

"Wednesday?" Mama Hemby quickly swallowed a mouthful of cake. "No, no, no, baby! We can't let down! Tomorrow—"

"Tomorrow? Tomorrow! Tomorrow's the funeral."

"After the funeral, we've got to go!"

Where do they "got to go" on the day of Uncle Pete's funeral? The freedom riders didn't know what to say. Neither did anybody else. But Mama Hemby's confident tone made you just want to say, "Yes, ma'am," like the freedom rider finally did. The only thing left to say was, "Who's going?"

"I'll go, after the service." Uncle Enoch's voice was quieting and low. He reached out and rubbed my shoulders, kissed my temple. "And look who's up now that it's time to go to bed!"

I smiled. "I'm hungry."

"You slept through dinner, Sleeping Beauty?"

"Supper too!"

"Well, there's plenty of food left. It's just put away."

There was plenty of food left, all right. The refrigerator was packed—a big ham, potato salad, corn on the cob, collards, chicken and dumplings, chicken roasted, chicken fried. I helped myself to potato salad, two fried short thighs, and a piece of the crumbly pineapple-coconut cake. They went on talking.

"Like Pete always said, we got to be consistent. We don't all have to go, just a few." Mama Hemby paused. "So who've we got now? Me, Enoch, Joseph Hicks . . ." That was the old man from Hendsonville.

Uncle Willie got up to leave. He was against all this from

the beginning, even before Uncle Pete made his freedom rider announcement on Easter Sunday.

"I'll go," he said, and shocked everybody.

"*You*'re going?" flew out my mouth before I could stuff it. I could have popped myself. He hadn't spoken or lifted his eyes to anyone since Uncle Pete had died. I wondered again what they were planning.

He cleared his throat yes, but didn't look back as he walked toward the door.

Aunt Minnie Ruth touched his arm quickly before he could leave, and asked, like a little girl, "Can I ride with you, Uncle Willie?"

He nodded and left.

Nobody breathed a word till Ma Pudnum said, "I'll—"

"No, Mama!" Mommy and Aunt Minnie Ruth yelled together.

"Can I go?" Nobody answered me. They were too busy trying to make sure that, wherever it was, Ma Pudnum didn't get there.

"Mama, that's too much. You need to rest."

"Now, Pudnum, you've got to be careful. You've got the Pressure, you know," Mama Hemby said.

"No, I believe I'm all right." She looked up from her hands lying on the table. "And I'm going to go." Mommy and Aunt Minnie Ruth looked at each other like "God help us."

"Then I'm going too," Mommy said.

I sat down in front of a plate almost as full as the refrigerator. No one had told me, but I knew they were planning to go to the courthouse to try and register—again. And I knew I should want to go, but I didn't. I had a fork full of potato salad right in front of my mouth, but as soon as it got in, all my taste for it, or for any of the other food on my plate, went away. I could see the dogs already. Tearing at Ma Pudnum? Mommy? No!

"Can I go?"

"No," Mommy said. "No need for you to go. You can't vote yet anyway."

"You can't vote down here."

"No. I vote in New York, but I'm going with Mama."

"Then I'm going with you."

She didn't say *yes*, but she didn't say *no*.

16 □□□□□□□□□□□□□□□□

Raindrops like stones pinged off a nearby rusting tin roof barn as we began the funeral procession into the church. A woman about Ma Pudnum's age tinkled out "What a Friend We Have in Jesus" on a mostly out-of-tune piano. Uncle Enoch escorted Ma Pudnum down to the front center pew. The rest of us followed. Mommy's knees buckled at the sight of the closed casket, and Daddy started to take her out, but she insisted she was fine—it was her legs that had the problem. He put his arm around her waist and carried her, feet barely grazing the floor, to our seats next to Ma Pudnum. Craig carried Ronnie, and Ronnie patted Craig's back. But worst was Uncle Willie. Aunt Minnie Ruth tried to hug the shame out of him, but he couldn't let it go.

I just wanted the whole thing over. My tears were already exhausted, and I was tired.

* * *

Songs and prayers started, but I only half joined them, since God, evidently, was only half-listening anyway. And I could only half believe that. There were billions of people on earth—and who knows who all else is out there clamoring for God's attention from other galaxies. How could I be upset if God didn't get to my request in time? *The problem is that, despite Sunday school book pictures, I never saw you as being somewhere with two eyes and ears, hastily meting out decisions to the universe. To me, you are more like blood, tending the whole body at the same time. I could understand the silence if you didn't know what was happening, or even if you* couldn't *do anything about it. But for you to know and* choose *silence, I'm sorry, but that's a bit much to have to be understanding.*

Hurt tears gripped my chest and clogged my throat, marking the loss of a once good friend. *From now on, I'll be polite to God, but that's it.* I sat, trying not to feel the pain of that decision, waiting for the long funeral to be over. After what seemed like hours of remarks and solos, the preacher rose to give the eulogy.

"I don't believe it," I thought out loud.

"Huh?" Craig said.

I've got one question, just one question, God. Whose side are you on? Nothing is hidden from you. You saw! You see everything! How can you stand for this? How long do we have to call before you pay us some mind? I always thought I knew, but maybe I've been wrong. So God, I've got to ask you. I've got to know. Whose side are you on?

"Funerals are for the living," the preacher went on. I looked around at the people who had packed the small church. Some of the students who had been at Ma Pudnum's house sat behind the deacons on the right side of the church. Debra Jean's boyfriends, Michael Evans and Melvin Jenkins, sat together along with other kids I remembered from the Easter Monday fish fry. I saw Miss Berry, their strict teacher, and others I didn't recognize. There were more, unable to fit into the church, paying final respects under umbrellas outside the church. I turned back around. The preacher was talking about living memorials. I hoped he wouldn't do it long.

I picked up a program. Uncle Pete's knock-out smile filled the center of the page. Above that in large capital letters were the words HOMEGOING SERVICE FOR PETER LAMONT JAMES, 1943–1963. Under that in bold letters was a scripture quotation: "I have fought the good fight, I have finished my race, I have kept the faith." II Timothy 4:7

"You came out to watch the sun rise? Is it doing something today it doesn't usually do?" He sits on the top step leaning against the porch beam, with his face set toward mixing colors in the sky. "That's the best thing about a day, and most people miss it most of their lives."

Violet swirling in myriad blues and pastel pinks supplanted all questions and fears for moments that stretched into yellow-glazed orange.

"Why don't you come to New York?"

He smiles and shakes his head. I understand. It's in him.

"Besides, too many buildings. Hides that right there." He points to the sun stepping through a ring of colors into a new day.

But the Lord is in His holy temple;
Let all the earth keep silence before Him.

Keep silence. Keep silence.
Keep silence before Him!

Habakkuk. I took a Bible from the seat in front and looked for the call to worship from Habakkuk that Uncle Pete and I had sung with the birds. *Keep silence.* Seems like God's doing enough of that for everybody. I fanned through the slew of minor prophets between Daniel and Malachi, the last book of the Old Testament. Habakkuk was there somewhere, I knew.

> The oracle of God which Habakkuk the prophet saw.
>
> O Lord, how long shall I cry for help and thou wilt not hear? Or cry to thee, "Violence!" and thou wilt not save? Why do you make me see wrongs and look upon trouble? Destruction and violence are before me; strife and contention arise. The law is paralyzed and justice never goes forth. The wicked surround the righteous, so justice is perverted.

Those were *my* questions! *Oh, God, Habakkuk asked the same things I did. What did you tell him? My sweet uncle is dead. What can you tell me?*

> Look among the nations and see; wonder and be astounded. For I am doing a work in your days that you would not believe even if you were told. . . .
>
> The vision awaits its time; it hastens to the end—it will not lie. If it seem slow, wait for it; it will surely come, it will not delay.
>
> Behold, whoever's soul is not upright shall fail, but the righteous shall live by their faith.

New tears came while I read. To tell the truth, I didn't understand it all. But I think I understood enough—for now anyway.

Hot tears mingled with rain on the six pallbearers' faces. Still, they and the other freedom workers sang strong and loud as Uncle Pete was lowered into the ground. This was Peter's favorite song, said a small brown girl who had cried softly and kissed Uncle Pete's lifeless hands during the viewing.

> "Well, I read in the paper
> Da-da, da-da, da-da
> Just the other day
> Da-da, da-da, da-da
> That the free—dom riders
> Were on their way
> Da-da, da-da, da-da
> And they're coming by bus
> Da-da, da-da, da-da
> And they're coming by train
> Da-da, da-da, da-da
> And they'll come by plane
> Da-da, da-da, da-da
> If you want them to
> Oh oh, Jim Crow, you never can kill us all!
> Oh oh, Jim Crow, discrimination's bound to fall!
> Oh oh, Jim Crow, you never can jail us all!
> Oh oh, Jim Crow, segregation bound to fall!"

After the funeral and feeding at the church, we all set out for the courthouse.

17 ◘◘◘◘◘◘◘◘◘◘◘◘◘◘◘◘◘

Uncle Enoch parked his pickup in front of the building. I looked for dogs. There were none. No police either. Just a few folk walking up and down Main Street, taking care of this and that, I guess. It was still early Monday afternoon.

Squeezed beneath half a dozen umbrellas, we walked up the six short steps to the county courthouse entrance in twos, trying to look natural. We didn't have a parade permit, and we didn't need to be getting arrested for something stupid like walking up the street. Inside, Uncle Enoch and Uncle Willie, dressed in Sunday shirts with suspenders and pants, took off their hats, then occupied their sweaty hands by fiddling with them while walking to a small desk marked REGISTRAR.

A small, middle-aged, brown-haired woman with cat-eye glasses looked up from her newspaper when she felt us in front of her desk. She scrunched her eyes and adjusted her rhinestone-decorated frames when she saw the group.

151

"Yes?" she asked, closing the paper. I heard other workers at surrounding desks whispering. "The nigras are back with that mess again," one said.

"Good morning, ma'am. We've come to register to vote," said Uncle Enoch.

But before she could answer, a big-bellied, sandy-brown-haired man appeared from the office behind the registrar clerk's desk, looking rather pleasant, and said, "What can I do for you people today?"

Uncle Enoch repeated our business. The man laughed a small, natural-sounding laugh, lowered his head, and ran his fingers through his crewcut. "Oh, well, I'm sorry. You can't do that today because the registrar only does that on Wednesdays."

"The full-time voter registrar only registers voters on Wednesdays, sir?"

"That's right. We're real busy around here with other important work."

I looked at the woman sitting at the desk. Her hands were clasped over the newspaper that she had just closed. There was not another piece of paper on her desk.

"Is this lady the registration clerk, sir?" Uncle Enoch asked.

"Yes, she is."

Uncle Enoch nodded toward the woman at the desk. "Sir, I don't see what work it is that she's doing. She was reading that newspaper when we walked in, and her sole activity since we've been speaking has been listening to our conversation."

"I . . . I . . . I . . ." the woman said.

Only for an instant, the fat-bellied man stopped smiling. "She's on coffee break," he said nicely. People from all over the building came out to gape and talk in small groups. He and Uncle Enoch faced off. I wanted to knock the smile off his face.

"We've been here every day for the last three weeks and have always been given some excuse for why this office can't register us. We're not leaving today unless we are registered," Uncle Enoch said, looking hard in that man's eyes.

Crewcut's smile faded, then came back. "Well, we're real busy, but what's your name?"

"James, Enoch James."

"Enoch, we're real busy, but since you-all have been coming down trying to register for so long, I tell you what I'm going to do." Crewcut acted as though he was getting ready to grant a big favor. "This is not the right time to do it"—*then when was*?—"but I'm going to bend the rules a little and let you-all take the test today."

A test to vote? In social studies classes teachers said all you had to do to vote was be a citizen, over twenty-one, and registered in your resident state.

Uncle Enoch thought and said, "Good."

Crewcut went away to get the tests.

"Uncle Enoch, what kind of test y'all got to take?"

"Literacy tests. You got to be able to read and write, know some history. We've been studying for it at the Freedom School."

Crewcut sauntered out of a back office with a handful of papers, and, two at a time, they were to take the mandatory literacy tests. For them citizenship, despite all constitutional claims I'd learned to the contrary, was not good enough for voting.

I watched Mama Hemby settle in to take the test. She

reached in her pocketbook and pulled out too-big reading glasses, which slid down to the end of her nose as soon as she put them on. When she read the first question, she frowned, then looked up angrily. I knew something big was wrong. She glanced over the rest of the paper, sucked her teeth, and sighed. Her eyebrows shifted up and down quickly; then she set her pen to write.

Uncle Willie was having an even harder time. His eyes narrowed, straining to understand the paragraph in front of him.

After ten minutes, Crewcut came back, still smiling, for the test papers. He took Uncle Willie's test first. "Willie, you didn't write anything but your name on this paper."

Uncle Willie was fidgeting with his hat again. "I'm not familiar with them laws you asked about." I looked over his shoulder. Crewcut had given Uncle Willie a paragraph of legal language that would have stumped a lawyer.

"Well, voting is serious business." Crewcut's smile was all gone now. "How can we let a person vote who can't even read and understand the law?" He tore up Uncle Willie's paper and threw it in a nearby trash can, with victory on his face. He picked up Mama Hemby's paper. His face turned red. "That's not the answer."

"Sir, that's an honest answer to a dishonest question," she told him. "The number of words in the Constitution is not what's important. What's important is what those words mean. I don't know the number of words in the Constitution, but I know that somewhere in there it says taxation without representation is not fair. And I'm seventy-five years old, been paying taxes all of my life, and have never been represented when laws are being made. I know what the words in the Constitution mean, but I don't know how many there are of them.''

"Well, until you do, you're not qualified to vote.'' He tore up her test paper too, and the pieces fell into the trash can. "Now y'all just get on out of here. We're busy. The registrar's office is closed.''

"We'll be back,'' Uncle Enoch said. We walked out, past whispers and acidic gazes, through the heavy mahogany doors, down the six steps in sets of two, across the street, and into the two parked cars.

I punched the back of the seat and cursed under my breath. No one spoke, but tiny Mama Hemby, squeezed between three people in the backseat, started singing a homemade song:

"The race is not given to the swift,
And I'm glad 'cause I can't walk that fast.
The race is not given to the strong,
And I'm glad 'cause that test I might not pass.
The race goes to the one who holds out to the end.
Hold out till the end, hold out till the end,
Hold out till the end.''

18 □□□□□□□□□□□□□□□□□□

The driver was no more than a year older than the Carter G. Woodson High School seniors that he picked up each morning on his school bus route. The school was usually his last stop, but the morning after the funeral, it was only his first.

Mommy had wanted another day with her mother. So on Tuesday, instead of going home, Craig and I hopped the colored bus to school with our cousins—only this day school wasn't on the agenda. About a month after they had started working at the Freedom School, Debra Jean and the students at Carter G. Woodson had started planning their own civil rights action. They were all too young to vote, but I guess they figured being able to get a cool drink at Hodges' without him having an ammonia fit would be nice. So they had targeted Hodges' for a sit-in. The day they had been planning for just happened to be the one after Uncle Pete's funeral. So Craig and I could go.

As the younger children filed off the front of the bus, about fifteen middle school and senior high students deftly snuck on through the back emergency exit, which hung ajar. Craig and I joined Debra Jean, Brenda, and other older students already on the bus, kneeling before the seats, being careful not to let our heads show in the window. The driver honked his horn and waved a greeting to Miss Berry, who stood smiling on the steps in front of the school. He drove off smuggling students to the Negro church in town. My blood raced.

The relatively large town church filled with students, a deafening silence, and a tinge of fear that went from breast to breast. It was a fear somewhat on the order of the kind before final exams, only more real. The outcome of this test could determine more than if we'd make our grade in September, but whether we made September at all.

It was sobering, humbling. When the organizer said, "Okay, somebody give me rule one," the Melvin Jenkins who answered was not Debra Jean's cutie-pie, two-timing ex-boyfriend that I'd met at the Easter Monday fish fry.

"Rule one. In a firm but polite voice, order something when the waiter asks you why you're sitting at the WHITES ONLY lunch counter. Order something very inexpensive in case they overcharge for spite."

"Good. Rule two."

The students' answers came back fast and sure.

"Rule two. Don't talk back if cursed or spoken to rudely."

"Three."

"Rule three. Sit up straight and don't slouch."

"Rule four. Don't laugh—it might be taken as an insult and divert attention from the real issue."

"Rule five. Don't curse."

"Rule six. If attacked, don't hit back. Escape if it comes to that. Otherwise, roll yourself up into a ball, bringing your knees and face together. Use your arms to cover your head for protection."

"Any questions?"

We sat in silence.

"All right. We've studied. We've trained. Y'all understand our mission. The only thing left is for us to do it. Remember the teachings of Jesus Christ, Gandhi, and Martin Luther King, Jr.—love and nonviolence. God be with you."

We walked over to Hodges' Five-and-Ten. There were no dogs. I felt a little better. And just before noon, the first set of protesters filled all ten of Hodges' lunch-counter seats. Craig and I didn't sit, since we had to head back to New York in the morning, but there was still important work for us. On the walls of the church office hung a chart that would be filled with the names of those in jail. That was our job, to confirm which students had actually been arrested. It was important to keep accurate track of the freedom riders, to make sure none "disappeared." I was glad I knew most of these kids from the Easter Monday fish fry.

A young woman who one of the kids told me was Helen Hodges' daughter-in-law Ginny asked the students at the counter, "What're y'all doing?" and it started.

"I'd like a Coke and fries, please," Debra Jean said politely to Ginny, whose face quickly flushed red with fear.

"We don't serve nigras."

"A Coke and fries will do, thank you," the boy next to Debra Jean couldn't resist saying. The frightened students bit their bottom lips to keep from laughing.

"Y'all know good and well nigras get fed around back. So if you want something, go there," she said. Nobody moved. "Paw! Paw, nigras are at the counter!" A fat man dressed in white came out of the kitchen—the same man who had wiped out the water fountain after Ronnie and I drank from it.

"What the hell is going on? Get out!"

"I told them to go around back!"

"No, I don't want these around back—I want them the hell out!" He started to come from behind the counter, I guess to throw them out, but decided to get help. He called the sheriff on the wall phone behind the counter while muttering "Niggers"—he didn't say *nigras* this time—"trying to take away all the white man's rights! Want to vote! Take over our schools! Well, not here you're not!"

I was not prepared for this. How did this man figure Negroes voting or drinking water from a public fountain took away his rights? For a moment, his belief didn't even make me angry, just amazed.

"Bob! Bob, this is Hodges. I got a bunch of niggers down here at my lunch counter demanding that I serve them. Now, unless the niggers done took over the country, I think I still got some rights. . . . Yeah . . . yeah, I thought so. See you in a few minutes, then." He turned back to the students. "Y'all are gonna be sorry you ever darkened my doorway!"

Meanwhile, the clock ticked past noon and Hodges' lunch crowd began to drift in. The clerks from surrounding stores and farmers coming from market were shocked when they saw us sitting at the counter. I heard a lot of them muttering the same kind of thing that Hodges man was saying.

But it wasn't until the would-be southern belle entered,

with a prim cover girl smile that flopped into a snarl when she saw the students at the counter, that real trouble began. She gasped. Her eyes teared. *Girl, please.* She changed her mind. Reaching past Debra Jean's shoulder, she grabbed the sugar jar that sat on the counter and emptied its contents onto one boy's head. He jumped, but Debra Jean's arms surrounded him, and he remembered. The crowd laughed. Ginny didn't seem to like the girl in general or her game in particular, knowing who was going to have to clean up after it. But the girl's eye landed on the maple syrup before Ginny thought to hide it. She was pouring it over the same guy's shoulders when the sheriff arrived.

A small knot of anger and fear formed in my belly.

"All right, your circus is over. Get up, every one of you!" he yelled. *"Now!"* No one moved. "Have it your way, then."

Brenda was first. I didn't want to see, but I couldn't not look. He pulled her off the stool and threw her in the direction of the door. She landed on her behind in front of the candy counter and slid the rest of the way to the door, stopping next to a pair of muddy shoes. I couldn't remember from the nonviolent resistance instructions if she was supposed to get up or not, but she did, and in a hurry, before those feet could begin stomping her.

"G'wine out," they said, pushing her. She resisted and was pushed straight up to the girl's face. She was older, but about the same height as Brenda. For a split second they searched each other's eyes. The girl's lips began to purse. *God, please don't let this girl spit in Brenda's face because if she does, Brenda's going to forget and slap her.* The girl swallowed, yelled something ugly, and helped push Brenda out the door.

Now outside, Craig and I watched the hideous madness grow like a wood-fed fire as more people entered the crowd. Grown white men scratched their heads and underarms and hopped around like gorillas, trying to shame the students by insinuating Negroes were apes. Fear and hate are not just words. They are a force. Fear grabbed for my heart and wrestled my mind. I caught Craig's hand. Something was reaching for Craig too—I could feel it. I sang aloud to ward off the evil. And as we sang, a ground swell of peace rose up from deep within us, allaying fear, quelling hate, freeing us to do what we had come to do.

Roughly the police pushed Melvin and Michael into the paddy wagon. As others followed, Craig called out their names, and I wrote them down in the palm of my hand. Brenda was already in the van.

"You got those names?" Craig asked.

"Yeah, but that's only nine. Where's Debra Jean?" I looked up in time to see the sheriff and another policeman carrying her to the van by her arms and ankles. She was still singing when they closed the van door. That was the last I saw of Debra Jean on this trip.

I believed for the students' safe return.

Craig and I ran back to the church to give the names of the students we had seen put into the police wagon to Iris, who was waiting at the church to phone them in to the student group's headquarters in Atlanta. That office, in turn, called the Salisboro sheriff and courts to inquire about the arrests—name by name. It was crucial that people outside of the county and even the state know about the arrests— and that the law inside the state know others knew. It was nothing new for Negroes to go into police custody and never come out alive—I knew that much from New York.

We spent the rest of the afternoon mimeographing fliers that described the day's events and announced a rally that night at the church, then riding all over three counties distributing them. On the way back we made a quick stop in to see Miss Luella, who had taken sick after the funeral. She was weak but was glad to see us.

By the time we got back, the church was rocking in song from the seven-thirty meeting that had just started.

"Uh-oh, Craig!"

"What?"

"We haven't called the house since we left this morning. Here it is night."

Craig sucked his teeth and shrugged. "They know where we were."

We were standing in the church office doorway when Uncle Willie walked in the door and headed for the sanctuary.

"Uncle Willie!" I hugged him tight. He kissed my head. We took seats in one of the last empty rows of the rapidly filling church.

"Y'all could have called," Mommy, leaning forward, whispered to me and Craig. She, Daddy, and Ronnie, along with Uncle Enoch, Aunt Minnie Ruth, and her daughters—except for Debra Jean and Brenda, who were in jail—filled the pew in back of us.

"You would have told us to come back," Craig said. Mommy rolled her eyes, sat back, and caught the song midverse.

The singing went on for hours. And with each chorus we became more certain of our task, our anointing, our victory.

19 □□□□□□□□□□□□□□□

Time had really flown since we'd returned to Brooklyn. With so much to do for the concert, sometimes it was hard to believe in all that had happened down South. No sooner had I given the concert program to Aunt Emma (she got the local printer to do it free), it seemed, than it was time to pick them up for the concert. Raspberry and I had walked sixteen Brooklyn blocks to and from Fulton Street to pick up final items for the concert, then gone, sweating and weighed down with packages, to the church. We put the flowers in the pulpit and the corsages in the refrigerator, and set up display tables for literature on voter registration and student civil rights groups.

We had hardly finished and gone home to change before it was six o'clock and we were back at the church for the concert. The church songbird floated in dressed like a canary. Really, you needed sunglasses to look at Aunt Emma for any length of time. She had donned a wide-brimmed yellow straw hat with huge tiger lilies around its band. A delicately crocheted skirt and top set neatly outlined her curvy body.

"Hey, baby." She kissed me on my forehead. "What can Aunt Emma help you with?"

I pressed tissue in my hands to absorb the sweat. "Hey, Aunt Emma. Everything's under control . . . I think."

"Sister Monroe, oh, good," Raspberry said, and brought out the corsage we'd bought for our mistress of ceremonies. He started out trying to pin it on her, but Aunt Emma's battleship breasts were intimidating. Instead, he stood there turning the corsage this way, then that, saying, "Huh, uh, uh."

Aunt Emma suppressed a laugh and said, "Why, thank you, I'll take care of that," then took the corsage.

Raspberry said, "Oh, good," then got lost quick. Aunt Emma and I looked at each other and cracked up. I had pinned the flowers just left and below her right shoulder when someone tapped my shoulder.

"Yes." I turned around quickly, right into Ma Pudnum, her face shining like the sun. Just like Mommy described from her dream.

"Grandma! Debra Jean and Brenda—"

"They're holding up fine, thank the Lord. I visited them yesterday," she answered before I could ask.

"In jail?"

She nodded and kissed me quickly. "But y'all are going to get them all out tonight." Her smile sobered to confident resolve. The processional music began, and the baritone line started out. "You better go on now."

"Yeah, I better," I said, but not moving.

"Go . . . go!" I ran and took my place with the altos.

Look at us, 125 strong, six rows of yellow and black. Craig and a football team, Raspberry and a baseball team. We were kids and we were powerful. No waiting till we were grown to matter. We could raise bail and send some freedom worker back to school *this* fall.

"Moving in the east!" the baritones belted, then, with a carefully rehearsed right foot lead and lean, the black-suited line moved up the aisle till they reached the front. They turned to face the audience.

"Moving in the west!" we altos and tenors cried, and moved out with the same step, except we had a left foot lead.

"Moving in the north!" The sopranos rose from their front row seats in the two far sections of the church. They marched toward each other, crossing at the middle section of pews, and turned to face front.

"Moving in the south!" Straight up the basses marched confidently in the two middle aisles.

> "God is moving
> By the Spirit!
> Moving in the land today!
> Signs and wonders!
> Yes, God's moving
> Move in us, we pray.
>
> God is moving
> By the Spirit!
> Do you know what you see?
> God is moving, God is moving
> Move, O, Lord, in me too!"

The twin soprano lines turned in opposite directions and marched into the choir loft behind the pulpit. Altos, tenors, baritones, and basses did likewise until we were all in, swaying together. Looking at Alton work the organ made me smile. His head, mouth open, beat out the meter of the march, while his tongue, as important to his playing as his long, ever-stretching fingers, darted out and licked his lips. The large organ swallowed most people, but Alton's tall, usually awkward, too-thin body was at home behind it. At first, Pamela's amplified piano chords worked hard to keep up with his rhythmic flow. When she finally looked up, he caught her eyes, smiled, and winked his approval. She shook her head and laughed; then she began to play in the new, improved way we had seen her grow into during our many rehearsals. Her head started going too. No one directed this song. Alton and Pamela signaled each other, then us to go into the final chorus.

The audience responded with thunderous amens and applause. We were shocked. I mean, we had done our best, but to be honest, our best wasn't that good. Hadn't they heard our mistakes? I had. I even heard Raspberry. I caught Pamela's eye to ask her. Her eyes were round as saucers. She tilted her hand in an so-so gesture, then shrugged. The anointing, it must be covering these folks' ears! We started laughing. The applause went on and on. They were still clapping when the velvety chords of our call to worship hymn began, reminding me of Uncle Pete and sunrise.

> "But the Lord is in His holy temple;
> Let all the earth keep silence before him."

Looking out over the choir and audience, I felt the same spirit that had so filled the Salisboro church after a day of sit-ins and arrests at Hodges' Five-and-Ten, that the singing couldn't stop but pressed on deep into the night. I remembered Debra Jean's face as she was loaded into the police wagon and the song that warded off fear and hate while Craig and I watched. I thought of Mama Hemby's homemade song in the back of a car, and rain pelting a freedom song meter against Uncle Pete's casket.

We sang ten songs, five back-to-back. Then Aunt Emma sang a solo and introduced Ma Pudnum, and the people from the civil rights groups spoke in the twenty-minute space before our second five songs. Aunt Emma took up the collection.

Including donations from local merchants, the concert brought in more than five thousand dollars.

At nine o'clock, just after the benediction, instead of being worn-out, we glowed and autographed one another's programs, wondering aloud about what we would do next. We talked about making the community youth choir concert an annual event, with the money going toward a Peter Lamont James Memorial Scholarship Fund, named for my sweet, strange uncle.

Darin, the twins, George, Parker, and I stayed to push away tables and get the church back to normal for morning service, then collapsed on the back pew into a new kind of tired that was anything but exhausting.

It was an energizing tired, an exhilarating tired—a sacred tired that empowered and whispered we were on a journey that would not end (nor had it really begun) with the concert. And it hinted of a lifetime of work that only our hands could do.

Beads of sweat made the fine hairs outlining Raspberry's upper lip visible. He felt me staring and opened his eyes, winked, then closed them again. I leaned my head back and closed my eyes too. And there, for a hair of a second, was Uncle Pete, smiling almost to the point of laughter. When his eyes met mine, he blew a kiss, then jutted out his chin in my direction as if to say, "That's for you." But before I could catch it, or scream "Wait a minute," or sigh "I miss you," he was gone, reviving a bittersweet, very real ache in my heart. He did not fade to gray but rather to an orangy glow that soothed like ointment.

The church sexton entered the room jingling his keys like Captain Kangaroo in the morning. We knew what that meant, and just as well. It was time to go. Outside, summer staked its claim on Brooklyn nights with a still heat, offering no breeze to cool my sweaty neck. The sexton jingled across the street to his home, and Raspberry headed toward his on Troy Avenue.

But I stood on the church steps under the floodlights with the program and the turbulent past three months that had produced it and forever changed my life.

Covering about two-thirds of the program's cover, and bleeding over onto printed letters, was the transparent head-and-shoulder silhouette of five young singers. Slightly lower and right of center was a stronger sketch of Uncle Pete's smiling face, taken from the same shot used for his funeral program. It was beautiful. For a full minute, I welcomed the idea of growing up, knowing art would be part of that future.

"Sheryl, are you going home tonight or tomorrow?"

The twins were waiting. I folded the program and put it in my pocketbook. There'd be time enough to think about the future; mine had already started with Mommy's dreams, Mommy's dreams and our Easter journey.